## HEAVEN-SENT

Bubaker said, "You're not fixing to leave Inferno anytime today, are you?"

"Not if I bed my horse for the night at your stable," Fargo replied, and grinned. "I'll want to get my ten dollars' worth."

"Good." Bubaker smiled. "Very good. Tend to him, then, and I'll look you up later so we can have us a talk." He paused. "What is it you do for a living, if you don't mind my asking?"

Fargo would have thought it was obvious. "I scout, mostly."

"Injun fighter?"

"Only when I've had to."

"Even better. I can't tell you how happy you've just made me."

"If you say so."

"You don't know it yet," Marshal Bubaker said, "but you could be the answer to our prayers."

# SIX-GUN INFERNO

by

Jon Sharpe

SIGNET
Published by the Penguin Group
Penguin Group (USA) LLC, 375 Hudson Street,
New York, New York 10014

USA | Canada | UK | Ireland | Australia | New Zealand | India | South Africa | China
penguin.com
A Penguin Random House Company

First published by Signet, an imprint of New American Library,
a division of Penguin Group (USA) LLC

First Printing, July 2014

The first chapter of this book appeared in *Colorado Carnage*, the three hundred ninety-second volume in this series.

ISBN 978-0-451-46804-8

Printed in the United States of America
10 9 8 7 6 5 4 3 2 1

PUBLISHER'S NOTE
This is a work of fiction. Names, characters, places, and incidents either are the product of the author's imagination or are used fictitiously, and any resemblance to actual persons, living or dead, business establishments, events, or locales is entirely coincidental.

# The Trailsman

Beginnings . . . they bend the tree and they mark the man. Skye Fargo was born when he was eighteen. Terror was his midwife, vengeance his first cry. Killing spawned Skye Fargo, ruthless, cold-blooded murder. Out of the acrid smoke of gunpowder still hanging in the air, he rose, cried out a promise never forgotten.

The Trailsman they began to call him all across the West: searcher, scout, hunter, the man who could see where others only looked, his skills for hire but not his soul, the man who lived each day to the fullest, yet trailed each tomorrow. Skye Fargo, the Trailsman, the seeker who could take the wildness of a land and the wanting of a woman and make them his own.

*1861—the sunbaked desert of southwestern Nevada, where a bullet to the brain is the least of a man's worries.*

# 1

The rider was a red-hot coal, his lungs a furnace. When he breathed, he swore he inhaled fire. The desert country of Nevada Territory was no place to be in the hottest month of the summer.

Skye Fargo drew rein and squinted from under his hat brim at the blazing source of his discomfort. "Where's a cloud when you need one?" he grumbled at the clear blue sky.

Fargo reached for his canteen but thought better of it. There was barely a third left and he had a lot of miles to cover.

A big man, broad at the shoulders, he wore buckskins and a white hat so coated with dust it looked to be brown. A well-worn Colt hung at his waist; a red bandanna added color to his neck. He swallowed, or tried to, and grimaced at how dry his throat had become. "The next time I say I want to take a shortcut," he said to his horse, "kick me."

The Ovaro twitched an ear. Head hung low, lathered with sweat, the stallion needed water more than Fargo did. Fargo patted its neck and said, "We'll get you a drink soon, big fella."

Or so Fargo hoped. The truth was, he'd decided to cut across a section of desert he'd never been through before, and now here he was, miles from anywhere, in the middle of an expanse of sand dunes and flats where the earth had been baked dry of life.

Fargo gigged the Ovaro into motion. He tried not to dwell on the last three creek beds they'd come across. The creeks ran with water only in the winter. Now they were as dry as his mouth.

The stallion plodded on.

Fargo bowed his head and closed his eyes. He imagined being in a saloon in the cool of an evening with a saucy dove on his lap and a bottle of Monongahela at his elbow. The woman was running her fingers through his hair and whispering the naughty things she'd like to do with him, but then a harsh voice intruded on his daydream.

"Where do you reckon you're goin', mister?"

Fargo snapped his head up and drew rein. "What the hell?"

There were two of them. Hard cases with six-shooters on their hips and suspicion in their eyes. Behind them were two horses. Neither the men nor their animals showed any sign of being withered by the sun.

"Can't you read?" the same man said, pointing.

Fargo looked, and blinked. "I must be sunstruck."

Someone had planted a sign. In painted letters it read INFERNO SALT LICK. TRESPASSERS WILL BE SHOT.

"Move along, mister," the second curly wolf said. "We won't tell you twice."

"My horse can use some water. There must be some hereabouts."

The first man stuck his thumbs in his gun belt. He wore a high-crowned hat and a vest that could use a cleaning. "Maybe there is and maybe there ain't. Turn that nag and light a shuck."

"I asked nice," Fargo said.

The second man gestured at hills to the north. "You see yonder? That's the lick. There's a spring. But Mr. Crillian, who runs things, doesn't let anybody take a drink except him and those who work for him."

"Which would be us," the first man said.

"If you want water," the second man said, and gestured to the east, "Inferno is about five miles thataway."

"Inferno?"

The man in the high-crowned hat snickered. "You have no notion of where you are, do you, buckskin?"

"Daniel Boone here must be lost, Clell," the second man joked.

"Dumb as a stump, Willy," Clell said.

They laughed.

Fargo's gaze fell on their horses, and on what was hanging from their saddle horns. "How much for one of your canteens?"

"They ain't for sale," Clell said. "Mosey on, or else."

"I'll pay you twenty dollars for one," Fargo offered.

"You don't listen too good, mister," Willy said. "You're not gettin' any water. You're on private property, and you've been told to scat."

"So scat," Clell said.

Fargo sighed. He looked at the blue sky and at the two guards and at the Ovaro, wearily hanging its head. Before the men could guess his intent, he swung down and took a step to one side, his hand brushing his holster. "Thirty-one dollars, but that's all I have."

Clell and Willy couldn't seem to believe their eyes.

"What does it take to get through that thick skull of yours?" Clell said.

"We want you gone, mister," Willy said. "We want you gone *now*."

"My horse needs water," Fargo said again.

"Tough," Willy said. "You can't make us give you any, not if we don't want to."

"Which we don't," Clell said. "Your critter can keel over, for all I care. Climb back on and make yourself scarce."

Fargo had no right to do what he was about to. But he was prickly where the Ovaro was concerned. Plus, he never could abide jackasses. "Either I pay you or I help myself. Your choice."

"Try and you die," Willy warned. "We'll give you to the count of three and then we will by-God gun you if you're not back on that animal of yours." He paused, and when Fargo didn't move, barked out, "One."

"To hell with that," Clell said. "You don't need to count. I'll settle his hash here and now." So saying, he stabbed for his six-gun.

# 2

Fargo drew and fanned a single shot from the hip before Clell cleared leather. The slug slammed into Clell's shoulder and spun him half around. Clell clutched himself and staggered, his revolver forgotten in the shock of being shot.

"You son of a bitch," Willy said.

Fargo covered him. "Unbuckle your gun belt and let it drop." He cocked his Colt as incentive.

Willy stared at the scarlet seeping between Clell's fingers and hastily did as he'd been told. "You've just made the worst mistake of your life. Mr. Crillian won't like this one bit."

"Disarm your pard," Fargo said. He was eager to check their canteens but he didn't want a bullet in the back.

"We'll be comin' for you, mister," Willy declared. "We'll find you and we'll bury you."

Fargo pointed the Colt at Willy's face. "Without the jabber, if you don't mind, and even if you do."

Muttering, Willy tossed Clell's gun belt.

Clell was still conscious, but his jaw was clenched and he quaked like an aspen leaf. "I'll kill you for this if it's the last thing I ever do."

"Sure you will." Sidling around them, Fargo stepped to a roan and slid the strap of the canteen over the saddle horn. He shook the canteen and smiled. It was half full. "Lie on the ground."

"The hell I will," Clell snarled.

"Either breathing or dead. Which will it be?"

Clell uttered a string of invectives, but he eased down with Willy's help. The pair lay there and glowered.

Fargo lowered the hammer and holstered the Colt. Opening the canteen, he took off his hat, poured the water in, and held the hat to the Ovaro's muzzle so the stallion could drink. "Here you go."

The Ovaro practically sucked it down.

"I hope that horse is worth your hide, mister," Willy said. "That's what this will cost you."

"Speaking of which," Fargo said. He jammed his hat back on, dropped the empty canteen, and fished in a pocket for his poke. Fingering out twenty dollars, he flipped the coins so they landed next to Clell. "For the water."

"We don't want your damn money," Clell spat.

"We want your blood," Willy said.

Replacing his poke, Fargo forked leather. "This Inferno you mentioned—it's a town, I take it?" A town he'd never heard of. Which wasn't unusual. New ones sprang up all the time.

"Go to hell," Willy said. "We're not tellin' you a thing."

"Is everyone there as friendly as you two?"

"Go to hell twice over," Willy said. "In the first place, we're not from the damn town. We work for Mr. Crillian and stay at the lick. And in the second place, if you're thinkin' they'll help you, they won't. They don't dare buck Mr. Crillian. He has them under his thumb."

"Do tell," Fargo said.

"He won't take this lyin' down," Clell said. "As sure as you're sittin' there, he'll send some of us after you."

"I'll tremble in my boots until then."

Clell spewed another string of obscenities. He was so mad, his face was flushed red and his veins bulged.

Fargo touched his hat brim. "Nice meeting you," he said, rubbing it in. Twisting, he made it a point to keep them in sight until he was out of rifle range. They didn't try to pick him off, though. Willy was busy bandaging Clell.

Reluctantly, Fargo brought the Ovaro to a trot. The sooner they reached the town, the sooner the stallion could have more water.

A pockmarked road led him to it. There looked to be three dozen buildings or so. Few were more than one story.

At the town limits was another sign. INFERNO. POP. 78. The 78 had a black line through it and below it was 61.

Few folks were out and about. An elderly woman in a bonnet regarded him as she might a rabid coyote. Several men outside the general store scrutinized him as if he were a hostile come to scalp their loved ones. Faces peered at him from windows and doorways.

Everyone Fargo saw had a haggard aspect about them.

He drew rein at a trough that had a few inches of dirty water at the bottom. Climbing down, he was about to let the Ovaro dip its head when a gun hammer clicked.

"No, you don't, stranger."

A gent with a tin star on his shirt had come out of a building with TOWN MARSHAL over the door. He had bristly eyebrows and a cleft chin, and he was pointing a shotgun. He also had the same worn-out look as the rest of them. From the way his clothes sagged, it appeared he had lost considerable weight recently.

"My horse needs it," Fargo said.

"Afraid I can't let you," the lawman said. "I'm Marshal Bubaker. Who might you be?"

Fargo told him.

"Well, Mr. Fargo, it's like this," Bubaker said, moving to the other side of the trough. "In case you haven't noticed, we're in the middle of a drought. The hottest damn summer anyone can recollect. It's so bad, we have to ration our water." He nodded at the dirty bit in the trough. "Even that sludge."

"Look at my horse, damn it."

"I can see he's tuckered. Put him up at the stable. It's ten dollars, but he'll get oats and enough to drink."

"Ten?" Fargo said. The amount was outrageous. It would leave him with a dollar to his name.

"Do you want your animal to have some water or not?"

Fargo frowned. "First Crillian's roosters, now this."

Marshal Bubaker stiffened. "Crillian, you say? What do you have to do with that vulture?"

"I had words with two of his men out near a salt lick."

"And you're still breathin'? If any of us from town goes anywhere near that place, they shoot on sight."

"One of them won't be doing any shooting for a spell," Fargo said, and turned to go up the street.

"Hold on," Marshal Bubaker said. "Why won't he?"

"He went for his gun."

"Well, now," Bubaker said, "this hombre have a handle?"

"Clell."

"I know him. He's supposed to be slick with a six-shooter. Not the quickest Crillian has working for him, but still." The lawman pursed his lips, then motioned at the trough. "Tell you what. Help yourself if you want."

"Why the change of heart?"

"Let's just say I want us to get off on the right foot. You're not fixing to leave Inferno anytime today, are you?"

"Not if I bed my horse for the night at your stable," Fargo replied, and grinned. "I'll want to get my ten dollars' worth."

"Good." Bubaker smiled. "Very good. Tend to him, then, and I'll look you up later so we can have us a talk." He paused. "What is it you do for a living, if you don't mind my asking?"

Fargo would have thought it was obvious. "I scout, mostly."

"Injun fighter?"

"Only when I've had to."

"Even better. I can't tell you how happy you've just made me."

"If you say so."

"You don't know it yet," Marshal Bubaker said, "but you could be the answer to our prayers."

# 3

The saloon was called the Sand Dune.

Several drinkers were at the bar and a couple of card games were under way. Everyone stopped what they were doing to stare when Fargo walked in.

The barkeep weighed enough for two men, yet he, too, looked as if he had been ill recently. He polished a glass and brought it and a full bottle over. "Here you go, friend. On the house."

About to reach for the bottle, Fargo stopped. "Are you drunk?"

The bartender chuckled. "I hardly touch the stuff, myself. No, Marshal Bubaker was in here and told me that anything you want is on the town."

"Well, now," Fargo said in amusement, "I should answer prayers more often."

"How's that again?"

"Nothing." Fargo scooped up the glass and bottle and turned to find a table.

"Anything you want, anything at all"—the bartender wasn't done—"all you have to do is ask."

"Are you passing out free money too?"

The barman snorted.

Fargo took a step and had a thought. "What about doves?"

The bartender leaned on an elbow. "I have two who work for me but they don't start until six. Can you wait that long? If you're randy and have to have a poke right this minute, I can send for one, but she's liable to gripe about having to work early and won't be in the best of moods. You know how contrary females can be."

"Six is fine." Fargo picked a corner table. He filled his glass and was savoring his first sip when the batwings creaked and in came Marshal Bubaker with a pair of well-dressed townsmen.

Bubaker looked around, spotted him, and made a beeline. "Fargo, I'd like you to meet Mr. Hoffstedder, our mayor, and Mr. Parkinson, our banker."

"I'm busy," Fargo said.

"It's important you talk to them," the lawman said.

"I just got here. It can wait."

Hoffstedder cleared his throat. He was on the scrawny side, with no more meat on him than a pencil. He also had the same worn-out look as the rest. "It's quite urgent, I assure you."

"Is everybody in town going to die in the next hour or so?"

"No. Of course not," Hoffstedder said. "What a silly thing to ask."

"Then it can wait."

Parkinson stepped forward. "Perhaps I should mention that you could earn a lot of money if you take us up on our offer." He had white hair and an air of self-importance.

"I'm not taking you up on anything for an hour," Fargo said, and wagged his fingers at the batwings. "Shoo."

"Show some respect," Marshal Bubaker said. "These are our leading citizens. You should feel honored."

Fargo drummed his fingers on the table. "I feel thirsty. I feel hungry. I feel plumb worn-out. I'm fixing to take it easy for a while. After I've liquored up and had some food, then, and only then, will we have our talk. If that's not good enough, you know where you can shove it."

"That was terribly rude," Hoffstedder said.

"Mister," Fargo said, "I'm nowhere near rude yet. But we'll get there right quick if you don't show some sense."

Parkinson angrily made as if to speak but Marshal Bubaker held up a hand.

"He's right. He just rode in, and it's plain he's been through hell. We've waited this long. We can wait another hour."

"I suppose," Hoffstedder said, although he didn't sound happy about it.

Bubaker steered them toward the batwings. As they went out, he smiled and waved.

"What is it about me that draws idiots like flies?" Fargo asked his bottle. He finished his glass and poured another and felt the weariness and some of the heat drain away. He was tempted to sit in on a card game, but he'd told the welcoming committee they could come back in an hour and he needed something in his belly.

Inferno had one restaurant. It was called Grandpa's. The man who ran it didn't look to be over thirty or very healthy. He wore a dirty apron and kept scratching himself as if he had fleas, but he cooked a fine meal. The tray he brought was heaped high with a platter of thick beefsteak and buttered potatoes, a bowl of gravy, and a side plate of bread.

Fargo's stomach growled at the prospect of hot food. He glanced around the table and asked, "Where's the salt?"

"There ain't any."

"You must have some in the back." Fargo had never heard of an eatery that didn't serve salt.

"None means none," the man said. "If I had some, do you think I'd look like this?" He pointed at his face.

"I don't savvy," Fargo admitted.

"Mister, the whole town ran out of salt a coon's age ago. What with the heat and all, it's made everybody as sick as dogs."

"So that's it," Fargo said.

The man looked down at himself. "I wish to God I had some."

"How does a town run out of salt?" Fargo wanted to know.

"It wasn't easy," the man said, and walked off.

Fargo remembered the salt lick, the no-trespassing sign, and Clell and Willy. No sooner did the thought cross his mind than the door opened and in walked Willy himself with two new hard cases.

Willy pointed at him and said something, and all three lowered their hands near their hardware.

# 4

A cold anger formed in the pit of Fargo's gut and spread like ice through his veins. He slid his right hand under the table as the three spread out with Willy in the middle.

"Bet you never reckoned on seein' me again," Willy said.

"Go," Fargo said, "and take your pards with you."

"You haven't even heard why I'm here," Willy said. "Mr. Crillian wants to see you. He sent me because I'd know who you were."

"No," Fargo said.

The man on the left had a scar on his cheek and a sneer on his mouth. "You don't have a say. What Mr. Crillian wants, Mr. Crillian gets."

The man on the right nodded. Or "boy" was more like it. He couldn't be much over sixteen. The Smith & Wesson on his hip looked too big for him to handle. "On your feet, mister. We're takin' you to him."

"No," Fargo said again.

"All Mr. Crillian wants to do is talk," Willy said. "He told me to be sure to tell you that."

"I don't give a damn."

The man with the scar said, "We'll drag you out if we have to."

"You can try."

The young one bristled. "You're not quick enough to gun all three of us before we'd gun you."

"Hold on," Willy said. "No one is gunnin' anybody. All Mr. Crillian wants to do is talk."

"He's comin' or else," the scarred man said.

"I have a meal to eat," Fargo told them. "Back up your big words or tuck tail."

"There won't be any gunplay," Willy assured him.

The man with the scar apparently had other ideas. "I heard what you did to Clell, but I'm not him. I'm a hell of a lot quicker."

Willy glared. "Nesbitt, damn it. Sheathe your horns. How many times must I say it? All Mr. Crillian wants is to talk."

"He can't talk if this hombre won't go," Nesbitt said. "We're takin' him to Mr. Crillian whether he wants to come or not."

Fargo had listened to enough. Unfurling from his chair, he said, "Start the dance or get the hell out."

"We're not here to shoot," Willy said.

"I'll start it, all right," Nesbitt spat.

"No!" Willy cried.

Nesbitt went for his six-gun.

Fargo drew and fanned two swift shots that smashed the tough guy back and toppled him like a chopped tree.

Nesbitt's mouth worked and a rivulet of blood trickled from a corner of his mouth. He gasped once and went limp.

"Hell!" the young one exclaimed.

"No shootin'! No shootin'!" Willy said.

Fargo twirled his Colt into his holster and said to the young one, "Do you want to dance, too?"

"You've done killed Nesbitt."

"He killed himself by being stupid. How about you? Are you a jackass, too?"

"Everybody calm down," Willy said. "This has gotten out of hand."

"I'm no jackass," the young one snarled. "And now that I've seen you draw, I think I can beat you."

"This Crillian must like to hire lunkheads," Fargo said.

With an oath, the young one streaked his hand to his Smith & Wesson.

Fargo's own hand was lightning. He slicked the Colt and fanned it once and a hole appeared in the boy's forehead. The would-be badman swayed and whimpered and buckled.

"It wasn't supposed to be like this," Willy said anxiously. "Mr. Crillian will have my hide. Hell, hell, hell."

Fargo pointed the Colt. "Your turn."

"Hold on!" Willy shrieked. "You heard me say no shootin'. It's not my fault they didn't listen."

"You brought them."

"Mr. Crillian told me to," Willy said.

"Then this is on him." Fargo sat back down but kept the Colt pointed. "Drag them out and throw them over their horses and take them to your boss with my regards."

"He'll be awful mad."

"Do I look like I give a damn?"

"You won't go back with me and talk to him?"

Fargo stared.

"I was just askin'." Willy stepped to Nesbitt, bent, and grabbed hold of Nesbitt's wrists. "You'd be doin' yourself a favor if you went."

"You don't know when to shut up, do you?"

"All I'm sayin' is that the next time Mr. Crillian might send six or ten of us. You can't shoot that many."

"I have plenty of cartridges," Fargo said.

"Damn, you have a lot of bark on you."

"Less jabber and more dragging."

"Fine. First you shoot my other pard and now you shoot these two. I can't say as I like you very much."

Just then the front door opened and in burst Marshal Bubaker. "I heard shots and . . ." The lawman stopped and gaped. "Hell in a basket. What's this?"

"He shoots everybody," Willy said.

"I've seen you before," Marshal Bubaker said. "You're one of Crillian's gun hands."

"I may give it up after all this," Willy said, continuing to pull. "Out of my way before he shoots me, too."

Bubaker moved aside and came over. "You're plumb hell on wheels, mister. But I reckon you know that."

"What I am is hungry," Fargo said. "How about if you keep an eye on Willy there while I eat?"

Willy was going out the door back-first, and heard him. "Don't worry about me. I'm not about to brace you. I know when not to push my luck. Dreel likely can take you, but I'm not him."

"Why am I still hearing you prattle?"

"I'm commencin' to hate you," Willy said.

"I'll watch him for you," Marshal Bubaker offered. "As much for the town as for you. Two dead is enough. Crillian will be mad enough to spit tacks. He might even raise his price."

"Price?" Fargo said.

"On the salt," Marshal Bubaker said. "It's already so high, we won't pay it. If it goes any higher, everybody in town will be up in arms."

"Good for them," Fargo said absently as he picked up the knife and fork. He couldn't wait to tear into the steak.

"You don't understand," Marshal Bubaker said. "It won't be Crillian they'll want to string up." He paused. "It'll be you."

# 5

All Fargo wanted was to eat his meal in peace. Despite himself, though, he was curious, and remarked, "I must have missed something."

"You've missed a lot," Marshal Bubaker said. "I'll explain in a bit." He turned and went out. When Willy came back in for the young gun hand, Bubaker was with him. Together they hoisted the body and carried it out.

After a while Bubaker returned. He closed the door, came to the table, and tiredly sank into a chair. "He's gone. I saw him ride out of town with my own eyes."

Fargo was chewing a delicious piece of steak and fat and didn't respond.

"In case you haven't figured it out yet, this whole business is about salt."

Fargo wondered if he should mention he had some in his saddlebags. Not much. He was running low and could stand to buy more.

"You've seen how sickly everyone looks?" Marshal Bubaker asked.

"Now that you mention it," Fargo said with his mouth full.

"It's because we haven't had any salt in months. And with the heat as bad as it's been, well . . ." Bubaker shrugged. "I never gave salt much thought before, but according to our doc, when you go without it for too long, all sorts of things happen. You get headaches. You throw up. You're tired all the time. You get cramps. And if you keep going without, you can die."

"Anyone died here?"

"Not yet," Bubaker said. "But the other night Mrs. Carmody had a fit. She flopped around on the floor with foam coming out of her mouth. The doc says it was a close thing."

"There's a salt lick five miles away," Fargo said.

Bubaker frowned and sat back. "That's where we would get ours if Mr. Jensen still owned it. But Crillian came in and took control. Him and his gun hands. Then he raised the price to ten times what it used to be. When we refused to pay, he cut us off and we've been cut off ever since."

"Back up," Fargo said. "How did he get control?"

"Crillian claims he bought the salt lick from Jensen and has a bill of sale to prove it." Bubaker's frown deepened. "But no one has seen Jensen since the sale took place. Jensen was an old coot. Ornery as hell. He was the first to settle in these parts. He liked living out there. Liked it so much, he was mad when the town sprang up. Had to about twist his arm to get him to sell us salt. I couldn't see him selling out. The whole thing is suspicious."

"You reckon?" Fargo said.

"Here now," the lawman said. "Suspicion ain't proof. I can't go out and arrest Crillian on a hunch."

"Why not send someone east for a wagon of salt to tide you over?" Fargo suggested.

"You think we haven't thought of that?" Bubaker retorted.

"We sent a man and never heard from him, so we sent another and never heard from him. I was against sending a third but everyone wanted to, so we did and he never came back, either."

"Crillian's doing?"

"That would be my guess. There's only one trail through the desert to the mountains and he might have men watching it." Bubaker tiredly rubbed his brow. "It's a fine mess we're in."

Fargo had another suggestion. "Arm every man in town and ride out to the salt lick and take it over."

"Crillian has pretty near twenty guns riding for him. We'd outnumber them, but no one in town is much shucks with a gun, and that includes me. They'd likely shoot us to ribbons."

"So you just wither away?"

Marshal Bubaker brightened. "Not if we can help it. And that's where you come in."

"I have about thirty minutes yet."

"Sorry?" Bubaker said.

"I wanted an hour, remember?"

"Oh. And here I am, bending your ear." Bubaker pushed his chair back and stood. "Sorry. I forgot, what with the bodies and all." He turned and walked out, his shoulders slumped in fatigue.

Fargo forked another piece of steak into his mouth. He had a fair idea of what they were going to ask of him. Should he or shouldn't he? That was the question. He had no personal stake in their fight. That they had let it go this far showed a remarkable lack of grit.

The owner ended Fargo's reverie by setting a saucer and cup down and filling the cup with piping hot coffee. "I would have brought this sooner but for all the lead flying around."

"They were on the prod," Fargo said.

"I saw the whole thing," the man said. "Fact is, I'm glad you gunned them. It's about time Crillian was taken down a peg or three. Or better yet, bucked out in gore."

"I'm not a killer for hire."

"Too bad. We could use one right about now." Wiping his hands on his apron, the man went into the back.

Fargo finished his meal in peace and quiet. He tried not to think about the town and all the people suffering from salt deprivation. He didn't know any of them personally. It was none of his affair. Except that twice now, gun sharks who worked for this Crillian had tried to put windows in his skull. Now *that,* he did take personally. He wasn't a cheek-turner and never had been. When someone tried to plant him, he was happy to return the favor.

His belly full, he was sitting there drinking coffee and musing when the door opened and in came Marshal Bubaker. He wasn't alone. With him were Parkinson, the banker, and a surprise—a woman.

Bubaker didn't mince words. "It's been an hour. Can we talk now? We have an offer to make you."

Fargo had made up his mind. "Let's hear it," he said.

# 6

The lawman pulled out a chair for the lady and she gracefully sat and showed her fine teeth in a warm smile.

"How do you do? I'm Melissa Gebhart. I'm pleased to make your acquaintance."

Fargo was pleased to make hers. She was an eyeful. Lustrous copper hair framed an oval face with bright green eyes, a slender nose, and lips as full as ripe cherries. Her dress had lace at the throat and at the sleeve cuffs. Pearl buttons ran from her throat to her middle. Her bosom would be the envy of many a female, as would her long legs. She was a vision, yet she, too, had the same haggard look as most everyone else.

Parkinson, the banker, cleared his throat. "Miss Gebhart runs a millinery shop and is very active in civic matters."

"You don't say," Fargo said. It was rare for a woman to involve herself in politics. Especially since women had yet to be allowed to vote.

"Tell him the other reason I'm here," Melissa said.

"It's hardly proper," Parkinson said.

"If you don't, I will," Melissa replied. When neither the banker or the lawman spoke up, she said, "I have a stake in this that goes beyond the salt. Ignatius Crillian has taken an interest in me."

"Ignatius?" Fargo said.

"It's not the least bit funny," Melissa said. "I've rebuffed him but he refuses to take no for an answer."

Her worry was genuine. It prompted Fargo to ask, "How far will he take it?"

"There's no telling. Any day now, he might have me carted out to the salt lick so he can have his way with me."

"Honestly, now," Parkinson said. "He's never laid a finger on you, and I doubt he would. There are limits, even for someone like him."

"If you say so," Melissa said skeptically.

"Extorting money from the town is one thing," Parkinson said. "He wouldn't dare force himself on you. The entire town would rise up against him."

"They haven't over the salt," Melissa said.

"Which is why we're here. Not because of your personal problem," Parkinson said. He turned to Fargo. "Let's get to it. We have an offer to make that you would be unwise to refuse."

"Is that a fact?" Fargo didn't like the banker much. The man put on airs.

"Let me handle this," Marshal Bubaker said.

"Get to it, then," Parkinson said.

"What's your hurry?" the lawman replied. Nonetheless, he folded his hands and said to Fargo, "You've stood up to Crillian's crowd twice now. That's more than any of us have done, as much as we might like to."

"They asked for trouble and they got it," Fargo said.

"How do you feel about giving Crillian more?" Bubaker asked.

Parkinson said, "You see, we're planning to wrest the salt lick from Crillian's control, but it has to be done right."

"We're not asking you to do our fighting for us," Bubaker quickly mentioned. "There are too many of them for one man to handle."

"What is it you want, exactly?" Fargo tried to get them to get to the point.

"We want our lives back," Parkinson said. "We want everyone hearty and hale. We want the damn salt that man won't give us."

"What we want of you," Bubaker said, "is to do what you do best."

"You want me to bed a dove?"

The lawman laughed. The banker pinched his lips in disapproval. The dress shop lady colored slightly, but smiled.

"That isn't quite what we had in mind," Bubaker said, chuckling. "You told me that you're a scout and you've tangled with

Injuns. And any hombre who goes into hostile country and makes it out again has to be as good as the Injuns are at sneaking around unseen."

"Ah," Fargo said.

"We'd like you to pay the salt lick a visit without Crillian knowing," Parkinson said. "Study the disposition of his forces, and how we can best take his small army by surprise."

"You make it sound like a war," Fargo said.

"It is," Bubaker said. "If we don't get our hands on some salt soon, a lot of people will die."

"Horribly," Melissa said.

"Will you or won't you help us?" Parkinson asked. "We'll pay you two hundred dollars for your trouble. You could leave as soon as you're done here and be back by morning with the information we need."

"That I can't do," Fargo said.

"Why not?" Marshal Bubaker asked, his disappointment obvious.

"My horse is worn-out, remember? He needs some rest. I can leave first thing in the morning. No sooner."

"Take one of our horses," Parkinson suggested. "Hell, I'll lend you my own animal."

"I'd rather use mine."

"But that will delay things," Parkinson said. "We desperately need the information to end our suffering."

"One more night won't matter much."

"My horse is a fine animal. Ask anyone. It will get you there and back with no problem."

"I'll ride my stallion."

Parkinson gestured in irritation. "Why are you being so pigheaded? A horse is a horse. One is as good as any other."

"Mine has saved my bacon more times than you have fingers and toes," Fargo said. "We've tangled with Apaches. With the Comanches and the Sioux. I know him as well as I know myself. I'm riding him and only him and not another damn word about it, or you can ride out there yourself on your fine animal and see how you do."

"No need to be huffy about it," Parkinson said.

"We've waited this long," Marshal Bubaker said to him, "we can wait a little longer."

Fargo had a thought. "Haven't any of you ever been out to the lick? Before Crillian took it over?"

"None of us ever had reason to," Bubaker replied. "Old Jensen always brought the salt in on his wagon."

"There's nothing out there but barren hills and the lick and the old man's cabin," Parkinson said. "Or so I've been told."

"You need to be careful," Marshal Bubaker advised. "If Crillian gets his hands on you, there's no telling what he'd do."

"Have you met him?"

The lawman nodded. "I've talked to him a few times. He's a strange one. Talks as if he's one of those cultured fellas. But he hires his gun out for a living."

"No one with any feelings for his fellow man could do what Crillian is doing to our town," Parkinson remarked.

Melissa had been quiet but now she stirred. "For my own part, I'd like to thank you in advance for risking your life on our behalf."

"Happy to help," Fargo said. He refrained from mentioning that his main reason for going was that twice now, Crillian's gun hands had tried to snuff his wick.

"Since you're not leaving until morning, you'll need a place to sleep tonight," Melissa said.

"Hadn't given that any thought yet," Fargo said.

She surprised him by saying, "How would you like to stay with me?"

# 7

It was considered unseemly, if not downright scandalous, for a single woman to invite a man to spend a night with her. Tongues would wag. Fingers would point.

The lawman looked startled. The banker scowled.

"I phrased that poorly," Melissa said, smiling. "I own my own house. I have a spare bedroom, and you're welcome to use it, if you'd like."

"I'm sure I can find a place for him to stay, my dear," Parkinson said.

"He could sleep in a cell at the jail," Marshal Bubaker said.

"Seriously?" Melissa said. "On one of those small threadbare cots? Behind bars?"

"I'd leave the cell door open."

"Miss Gebhart's place is fine," Fargo said, trying to make it sound as if he didn't care one way or the other when secretly the notion of being alone with her set him to tingling down low.

"People might talk," Parkinson said.

"Let them," Melissa said. "I'm a grown woman and can do as I please. My reputation speaks for itself."

"You're a perfect lady," Parkinson said. "And it's considerate of you to open your home to him. But are you thinking this entirely through?"

"How do you mean?"

"What if Crillian hears about it?" the banker said. "He has his heart set on you and won't take it kindly."

"As if I give a good damn what Ignatius Crillian thinks," Melissa said. "And it's not his heart so much as another part of his anatomy."

Marshal Bubaker chuckled. "I like how you put that, ma'am."

"I was only saying," Parkinson said. "The last thing I'd want is for Crillian to be mad at me. I imagined you'd feel the same."

Fargo came to her defense with, "He'll be mad as hell when you attack the salt lick."

"Not if he's not there," Parkinson said. "Which brings me to a pertinent question. Would you be willing to assassinate him for us?"

"What?" Melissa said.

"You didn't mention that when we talked about coming here to talk to Fargo," Marshal Bubaker said.

"It just came to me," Parkinson said. "In one fell swoop, the scout here could solve all our problems."

"I don't hire out my gun to kill," Fargo said.

"You're going there to spy for us. You're bound to see him. One shot is all it would take. And instead of two hundred dollars, I'll pay you five hundred out of my own pocket."

"Oh, Mr. Parkinson," Melissa said.

"Don't 'oh' me," the banker said. "I'm being practical. You make it sound like a bad thing when we all know Crillian will have to be eliminated. What difference does it make if we kill him when we attack the lick or if the scout does it for us?"

"The scout has a name," Fargo said.

"No offense meant, I assure you," Parkinson said glibly, and pressed him with, "What do you say? Five hundred dollars is a lot of money. It could keep you in whiskey for a year."

"Not the way I drink."

"Yes or no?"

"No," Fargo said. There were lines he wouldn't cross and that was one of them. He would kill when he had to, but that was as far as he would go. To go any further would make him no better than the outlaws and riffraff who gunned folks down for the hell of it.

"How unfortunate," Parkinson said. "You could have made things so much easier for us."

"He's helping enough as it is," Marshal Bubaker said.

"Without a doubt," Parkinson said, but he didn't sound as if he truly believed that.

"Then it's settled," Melissa said. "I'll take him to my place as soon as he's done eating, and after a good night's sleep he can be on his way."

Fargo refilled his coffee cup and sat back to give the impression he was in no hurry to leave.

"Well, I have things to do," Marshal Bubaker said, rising. "I'll be in front of my office at dawn to see Fargo off."

"As will I," Parkinson said. He stood, too, but hesitated. "Are you absolutely positive I can't change your mind about having him stay with you?"

"Mr. Parkinson, please," Melissa said.

"It's your life," the banker said. With a bow of his head, he trailed off after the lawman.

"Sometimes I don't know what to make of him," Melissa remarked. "He asked me out once. The mayor has asked me out several times. And now Crillian comes along."

"All these gents show an interest in you, and you invite me to spend the night," Fargo said.

"Don't make more of it than there is." Even though they were the only two there—the cook had gone into the back—Melissa bent toward him and said in a hushed voice, "To tell the truth, I have a secret reason for inviting you."

"You can't wait to get your hands on my body?"

Melissa laughed. "Goodness gracious, no."

"You want to take a bath together?"

"That would be fun, but no." Melissa gazed at the front door. "No, I asked you over because I'll feel safer with you there."

"Safer from Crillian? The banker? Or the mayor?"

"You might think this is silly of me, but for a while now I've had a feeling that I'm being watched and followed."

"I learned a long time ago not to take a lady's intuition lightly," Fargo said.

"Thank you for that. And for doing me the favor of staying with me. I can breathe a little easier. For a while, at least."

It struck Fargo that she was genuinely afraid. "You're pretty rattled by all this, aren't you?"

"I admit to a certain nervousness," Melissa said. "I keep thinking that maybe it's all in my head. That I'm feeling so poorly on account of not having any salt, that I'm imagining things. The other night I had a nightmare where Crillian had me abducted and carted off against my will. That's why I mentioned it earlier."

"Anyone tries to cart you off," Fargo said only half in jest, and patted his Colt, "they'll answer to me."

"It's difficult being a single woman out here," Melissa said. "There are so few of us, we have suitors crawling out of the woodwork."

"Men can be randy goats," Fargo admitted.

"I don't like that much. I don't like being pressured. It's my virtue and I'll do with it as I please."

"I'm happy to hear you say that," Fargo said.

"You are?"

"I'm hoping that before the night is over, your virtue and me will become better acquainted."

Melissa blushed, and looked him in the eyes. "You never know. Give it a try and see what happens."

# 8

Inferno lived up to its name. The late-afternoon sun turned the town into an oven. Hardly anyone was out and about. Dogs had taken shelter in the shade, and cats were too smart to even step outside.

Fargo's buckskins clung to him before they went a block.

Melissa walked briskly, her dress swishing, squinting against the glare. "This heat is atrocious. I don't know why I stay on here. I honestly don't."

"You must like to sweat."

"I like small towns better than big towns. I like the quiet."

"There are lots of small towns," Fargo said. "How did you end up here?"

"I was with a party of people bound for southern California. We stopped to buy supplies and I walked around. It was so peaceful and everyone was so friendly, I decided to stay." She paused. "Of course, it was in the spring and not nearly as hot. If only I'd known."

"You can always leave."

"I suppose. But once you've set down roots, it's not so easy to tear them up again."

"I wouldn't know," Fargo admitted. He liked to wander where the wind took him. To feel the thrill of never knowing what lay over the next horizon.

"You've never wanted a wife and children and a home of your very own?"

"Never."

"I envy you," Melissa said, "but I could never be you. I enjoy a settled life. Four walls and a roof give me a sense of security."

Town life would smother Fargo. The same four walls day after day would close in and he would feel trapped. Give him the wide open spaces.

"You have an adventurous spirit," Melissa said. "I admire that."

Fargo happened to glance at a store window they were passing and caught sight of a man across the street walking in the same direction, and staring at them. He glanced over and the man looked away. "Well, now."

"What?"

"Nothing," Fargo said. He didn't want to worry her. The next window he looked into, there the man was, continuing to pace them. Their shadower wore a store-bought suit and a bowler. "Any other gents around here have an interest in you, besides the banker and the mayor and Crillian?"

"I told you, they come out of the woodwork. A lot don't say anything, but a woman can see it in their eyes."

"Any you have an interest in?"

"Not a great interest, no. Although there are one or two I've let take me out to eat on occasion."

"Would one of them be about five feet tall with big ears and a nose as long as your arm?"

"Goodness, I should hope not," Melissa said, and laughed. "Long noses do nothing for me."

Fargo decided to find out if the man across the street was shadowing them because he was an admirer of hers. "Do you like meat?"

Melissa stopped and faced him. "What in the world does that have to do with anything?"

Fargo nodded at the next building. In large letters across the front was FRANK'S BUTCHERY. FRESH MEATS DAILY. "Let's go in."

"I'm not interested in meat at the moment."

"Yes, you are." Clasping her elbow, Fargo steered her inside. She didn't resist but she looked terribly confused. A customer was being served and two others were waiting their turn. "Whatever you do," he whispered in her ear, "don't leave until I get back."

"You're leaving me?"

Fargo moved toward the far end of the counter and around it to a door.

"Hold on, there," the butcher said. A brawny slab with a paunch, he wore a body-length apron with red smears. He was holding a cleaver. "Where do you think you're going?"

"You have a back door?"

"Sure I do. But no one goes back there but me." The butcher took a step, the cleaver at his side.

Fargo placed his hand on his Colt. "You ever hear the one about the gent who brought a knife to a gunfight?"

The butcher glanced at Fargo's six-gun. "What do you want to go out the back way for?"

"I have to. I won't touch anything. I promise." Fargo went through. He glimpsed a table with a side of beef dripping blood and the haunch of an antelope hanging from a hook and other chunks and strips, and then he was at the back door and shoved it open.

After being inside, the bright sunlight hurt his eyes. Hurrying to a side street, he jogged to Main. Careful not to show himself, he peered around the corner.

The small man in the bowler was directly across from the butcher shop, watching it.

Pulling his hat low, Fargo was about to cross the street and hope the man didn't notice him, when a buckboard approached. He waited until it was between him and the watcher, then sprinted in front of it to the other side.

The driver spoiled things by shaking a fist and hollering, "You jackass! I nearly ran you down!"

The small man in the bowler looked over at them. The instant he set eyes on Fargo, he turned and bolted.

Fargo went after him. He was fast on his feet but the small man pulled ahead, came to a corner, and flew around it. When Fargo reached the same spot, the side street was empty.

"Damn."

Fargo moved down the middle of the street, glancing into every window, at every doorway.

The exertion had him sweating worse than ever. Some drops trickled into his eyes and stung, and he mopped at them with his sleeve.

That was when a gunshot cracked.

# 9

By the sound, it was a derringer.

Fargo felt his hat shift on his head as he dropped into a crouch and palmed his Colt. The shot had come from the right side of the street but he had no idea where. None of the doors were open. No one was visible in any of the windows. He stayed crouched, thinking the shooter would try again, but nothing happened.

Boots pounded, and up the street came Marshal Bubaker, his own revolver out. "What's going on?" he demanded. "I was making my rounds and heard a shot."

Fargo told him about the try on his life. Taking off his hat, he found a crease where it had been nicked.

"You were lucky," the lawman said. "A little lower and you wouldn't be breathing. Did you see who took the shot at you?"

Fargo described the small man in the bowler.

"Big ears and a big nose, you say?" Bubaker said, his brow furrowed. "I can't say that rings any bells."

"In a town this size?" Fargo said skeptically. By rights, the lawman should have been acquainted with everyone in it.

"I'm telling you I can't think of anyone with big ears and a big nose who goes around all dandified," Bubaker insisted.

Fargo shoved the Colt into his holster.

"It could be one of Crillian's men," Bubaker said. "Gussied up so we won't recognize him for what he is."

Fargo hadn't thought of that. It would explain Melissa's feeling of being watched. "This Crillian sounds like a real bastard."

"He's no daisy," Bubaker said.

They drifted toward Main Street, Fargo checking windows and doorways, just in case.

"Matter of fact," the lawman said, "a word to the wise, if you don't mind."

"I'm listening," Fargo said.

"You've shot three of Crillian's men now. He'll want to return the favor."

"I don't gun easy."

"Some will come at you straight-up, like they did at the restaurant. I wouldn't put it past a few of the others, though, to do it in the back."

"Any I might have heard of?" Fargo asked.

"None I had. Except for one. He goes by the handle of Dreel. A two-gun man. Cross-draws instead of the usual or a flip draw. Word is, he's the best killer of the bunch."

Fargo vaguely recollected hearing of a gun hand by that name from down Texas way.

"There's also a Mex," the lawman went on. "Ramirez, his name is. His thing is knives. He can stick one in a fly on a wall at ten paces. Or so they say."

"Dreel. Ramirez. Thanks for the warnings."

They reached Main Street. Fargo looked toward the butcher shop and spied Melissa Gebhart out in front, waiting.

"There's one other worth mentioning," Bubaker said. "His name is Werner. Big German fella. Has fists the size of hams. He's powerful fond of breaking bones. Wears a six-shooter, but it's those fists you have to watch out for."

"Again, I'm obliged." Fargo started up Main. "I have to go see a lady. Watch your own back."

"Always," Bubaker said.

Anxiously wringing her hands, Melissa came to meet him. "Thank goodness you're all right. I thought I heard a shot."

"You were supposed to wait in the butcher shop."

"I was too worried," Melissa said.

"You hardly know me."

"True, but you've taken our side, and I wouldn't want you hurt on our account," Melissa said, sounding sincere.

Fargo took her arm. "Where's this house of yours?"

"Not far." She started off. "Tell me what happened."

Fargo did, ending with "It could be he's been watching you for a while. It would explain that feeling you have."

"I'm surprised I didn't notice him myself," Melissa said. "But then, I'm afraid I don't pay much attention to what's going on around me. I've heard that's a female trait."

"I've met men who go around deaf and dumb, too," Fargo said.

"'Dumb' is a little harsh, don't you think?"

"Not if it gets you killed."

"You're not one for mincing words, are you? It must get you in trouble a lot."

If she only knew, Fargo thought. A friend of his once joked that if he'd learn to keep his mouth shut, he'd live longer. "Let's just say a lot of folks have no sense of humor."

"Ignatius Crillian doesn't."

"Figures."

Melissa squeezed his arm. "If that man in the bowler does work for him, word will reach him right quick about you."

Fargo thought of Clell and the pair in the eatery. "Word already has."

"You be careful, hear? I wouldn't want anything to happen to you."

"Makes two of us," Fargo said.

# 10

Her house was small and well maintained, and as Melissa proudly remarked, hers and hers alone.

Fargo understood her pride. Few single women owned their own homes. For one thing, jobs were hard for women to come by. For another, those they did find seldom paid well.

Melissa led him down a hall to a parlor. There was a settee and a couple of chairs, and a cowhide rug in between. "Make yourself comfortable. I'll fix refreshments. Do you like tea?"

"The only way I'd ever drink it," Fargo said, "is if someone pours it down my throat after I'm dead."

Melissa laughed. "Coffee, then."

"Whiskey would be even better."

Melissa hesitated, then said, "I'm not sure that would be wise. Liquor tends to lower my inhibitions."

“It doesn’t lower mine.” Fargo grinned. “I don’t have any.”

“Coffee it is,” Melissa said, and whisked out.

Fargo sighed and roosted on the settee. He thought about how nicely she filled out her dress, and how they’d have an entire night to themselves, and the hint she had dropped earlier about becoming better acquainted.

He noticed a china cabinet in a corner. It didn’t contain many pieces. On a wall was a painting of an outdoor scene, a mountain capped with snow. Whoever the artist was could stand to improve.

He leaned back and gazed about him again. He happened to look toward the window and saw an eyeball peering back at him. Without letting on, he went on idly gazing about as if he were bored. He let over a minute go by, then stood and moved to the hall and down it to the kitchen.

Melissa was at the stove. She had put a pot on to brew and was taking sugar from a cupboard. “Skye,” she said as if surprised. “You got tired of waiting?”

Fargo put a finger to his lips and stepped to the back door. Quietly throwing the bolt, he slipped out and along the house to the side. A quick peek filled him with grim resolve.

It was the small man in the bowler, only the bowler was off. The man was still peering in the parlor window.

Placing his hand on his Colt, Fargo stalked toward him.

The small man rose onto the tips of his toes and craned his neck, evidently to try to see down the hall.

Easing the Colt out, Fargo raised it shoulder-high, the barrel pointed at the sky. Another fifteen feet and the skulker with the big ears and big nose was in for a headache.

The man sank onto his heels and put a hand on his hip.

The next moment, something crunched under Fargo’s boot.

The small man whirled. Where most would have run, he did the unexpected. He threw his bowler at Fargo’s face.

Fargo instinctively swatted at it to keep it from hitting him, and in the instant he took his eyes off his quarry, the small man did an incredible thing. Namely, he leaped straight up and kicked Fargo in the chest.

Fargo was knocked back. He recovered, but the small man was racing for the front of the house. Fargo took aim but didn’t shoot. He never could bring himself to shoot someone in the back. With an oath, he gave chase.

The small man bounded around the corner, glancing over his shoulder as he did. He was grinning.

"Son of a bitch," Fargo said under his breath, and concentrated on overtaking him. When he reached the front yard, he was taken aback to discover that, once again, the small man had seemingly vanished into thin air.

"Where the hell?" Fargo said, turning right and left. There was nowhere for the man to hide. The brown grass was cropped close. A single rosebush had withered and was virtually without leaves.

Fargo ran to the street and looked both ways.

Once again, nothing.

Fargo swore some more. This made twice the man in the bowler had gotten the better of him. He went up the street a short way. The only person he saw was a white-haired townsman in a rocking chair, smoking a pipe.

Disgusted, Fargo returned to Melissa's. She was out front, holding the bowler the man had thrown.

"I followed you. I saw him run away."

Fargo realized he was still holding his Colt and holstered it. "Did you recognize him?"

Melissa shook her head. "I never set eyes on him before." She held out the bowler. "What do you want to do with this?"

Fargo took it and turned it over and looked inside. Dropping it on the ground, he raised his right leg and stomped it flat.

Melissa snickered. "That'll teach him."

"He put a crease in mine," Fargo said. "I'm returning the favor." For good measure he stomped on it again, picked it up, and tossed it out in the street.

"The coffee should be about ready," Melissa said.

As they went inside Fargo gave the street another scrutiny but, save for the old man smoking his pipe, no one else was abroad.

"You nearly caught him that time," Melissa commented. "I should think you've scared him off for good."

Fargo doubted it. The small man hadn't shown any sign of being afraid.

The aroma of the percolating coffee filled the kitchen. Melissa bid him to take a seat while she got a cup and saucer from a cupboard, and poured. She brought sugar and a spoon, as well.

"I wish it were salt," she said as she set them down.

"With coffee?" Fargo said.

"You know what I mean." Melissa sat across from him and folded her arms on the table. "I've been having dizzy spells of late. Now and then my vision blurs, too. It's scary."

Fargo had left his saddle and saddlebags at the stable or he'd give her the little salt he had left then and there. He made a mental note to give it to her later, and spooned sugar into his cup. "How bad off are some of the people hereabouts?"

"Some are so weak they can't get out of bed. No one has died yet, but it's only a matter of time."

"One of you should have put a slug into Crillian when this whole mess began," Fargo remarked.

"The folks here are peaceable," Melissa said. "Most wouldn't harm a soul. Even Marshal Bubaker."

"So they'll let themselves suffer?"

"Crillian has legal claim to the salt lick. Or says he does. He has the right to sell the salt at any price he wants."

"You're making excuses for him now?" Fargo said in amazement.

"I'm just telling you how things are." Melissa bowed her head. "All I want is to have this nightmare over with. One way or another." She looked up. "And if we can't do it, it's up to someone like you."

"Lucky me," Fargo said.

## 11

Melissa was in a talkative mood. She related her childhood in Indiana. She told him how she had always wanted to see the West. Tales of the mountains and the prairies had fascinated her.

"So you live in the middle of a desert?" Fargo said at that point.

Melissa laughed. "What can I say? There's something about the sand dunes when the stars shine on them at night."

"If you say so." Fargo was about as fond of deserts as he was of swamps. He hated swamps.

"From all accounts, Mr. Jensen felt the same way. It's why he settled out at the salt lick. I'll never believe he sold out to Crillian. I bet the poor man is buried out in those hills." Agitated, she stood and moved to the window. "If you could find his body when you're out there, the marshal could arrest Crillian and we could put him on trial."

"Unless you have a bloodhound handy, how exactly would I find it? I doubt Crillian put up a headstone."

"I know. I'm grasping at straws. I just don't want any more blood to be shed."

"I can't make any promises there," Fargo said.

"We've suffered so much for so long." Melissa turned and took a step and drew up short. Her palm rose to her brow and she closed her eyes and swayed. "Oh my. Another bout. The worst yet." She began to topple.

Fargo was out of his chair and caught her before she hit the floor. Sweeping her into his arms, he carried her from the kitchen to a room midway to the parlor and pushed the door open with his foot. It was her bedroom. She'd pointed it out to him earlier. Crossing to the bed, he carefully deposited her on a pink quilt, saying, "You should rest a spell."

Melissa was woozily moving her head from side to side. With an intent effort, she focused on him and said weakly, "This isn't necessary. I'll be on my feet in a few minutes as good as new."

"Liar," Fargo said. He put a hand to her forehead. She wasn't running a fever but she was caked with a cold sweat.

"It's the lack of salt," Melissa said. "A lot of people are a lot worse off than me."

"Rest," Fargo said. "I'll be back in five minutes or so." He stepped to the door, but she called his name.

"Where are you going? If it's supper you want, I'll cook a meal as soon as I'm back on my feet."

"It's something else," Fargo said. "Stay put. And this time I mean it."

"You're sure a bossy cuss," Melissa said, but she smiled.

Fargo hastened out and down the street to the stable. He was thinking of Melissa and the salt in his saddlebags. The last thing he expected was for the small man with the big nose and big ears to appear from between two buildings holding a derringer.

"Remember me?"

Fargo stopped. He was tempted to go for his Colt but he wasn't hankering to take a slug. "Looking for your headpiece?"

"For you," the small man said. "The man I work for gave me new orders."

Fargo didn't think there had been time for the small man to get to the salt lick and back again. "Crillian is here in town?"

"Is that what you think?"

"That he has you keeping an eye on Melissa Gebhart. Everyone knows he's interested in her."

"Interesting," the small man said. He had a faint accent to his voice that Fargo couldn't quite place.

"What are your orders?"

"I'm to take you for a ride."

"Where to? The salt lick?"

"That's as good a place as any, I suppose," the small man said.

Fargo wondered what he meant by that. "I would like a word with this boss of yours about the salt."

"Talking to him won't do any good," the small man said. "He won't hand any over until Inferno comes to its senses and pays him what he's asking."

"People are sick," Fargo said. "Melissa Gebhart is having fainting spells."

"That's of no matter to me." The small man wagged the derringer. "Enough small talk. Keep your hands where I can see them and follow me down this alley."

"So you can put a slug into me? No, thanks." Fargo would rather have their scrape right there.

"This derringer is so you don't shoot me," the small man said. "If you behave yourself, all we'll do is ride."

"To where? The lick?"

"You'll see."

"My horse is in the stable," Fargo said.

"I have mine and an extra waiting. Yes or no? It will be worth your while to come."

Fargo had half a mind to go with him. He'd see the salt lick up close without having to risk his hide sneaking in. But he very much doubted Crillian would let him leave again. Not in one piece.

"Shed your hogleg first."

"I can't keep it?"

"Do I look loco?"

Fargo made a show of extending a thumb and finger and slowly reaching for his Colt. His hand was an inch above it when he glanced to his left and said, as if surprised, "Marshal Bubaker. What are you doing here?"

The small man gave a start and backpedaled, blurting, "The tin star? Where?"

In two long bounds Fargo reached the building on the right. Drawing his Colt, he poked his head out.

The small man was racing down the alley. He looked back and thrust his derringer toward him.

Fargo jerked from sight but there was no shot. When he looked out again, the small man was going around the far end. He'd been tricked.

Instead of running after him, Fargo flew up the street to the next junction and along a side street to the rear.

Once again, the small man was nowhere to be seen.

"Damn it to hell," Fargo fumed. He searched for tracks but the ground was too hard.

Determined to find him, Fargo roved up one street and down another. Ten minutes of searching proved fruitless.

"Next time," Fargo growled.

The stable doors were wide open to admit what little breeze there was. Even so, it was almost as hot inside as outside.

Fargo's saddle was draped over the stall, his saddlebags and bedroll in it. No one could get at them without the stallion kicking their lights out. He stuck the salt in a pocket, retied the saddlebag, and was out in the sun again with no one the wiser.

He stayed alert for the little man with the derringer but made it to Melissa's without incident.

She had fallen asleep.

Reluctant to disturb her, Fargo took the salt to the kitchen and placed it on her counter. A check of her pantry turned up eggs and a strip of hog meat. It would make great bacon.

After firing up her stove, he rummaged in her cupboards and drawers for plates and silverware and the like. He found a butcher knife, cut the hog meat into strips, and laid them out in a frying pan. Soon the kitchen filled with the smell of sizzling fat. When the bacon was about done, he broke ten eggs and scrambled them. He also made toast.

Melissa shuffled into the kitchen as he was setting the food out, sleepily rubbing her head. "What's this?"

"You need to get your strength back."

"You cooked for me?"

Fargo pulled out a chair. "I'd have brought a tray."

"Aren't you the perfect gentleman?" Melissa teased. She spied the salt and gave a start. "What's that?"

"For you," Fargo said. "The last of mine."

"I couldn't."

"The hell you can't. You're the one who needs it."

Melissa's eyes filled with tears. Coming over, she embraced him and whispered in his ear, "Thank you."

Fargo had her sit. She ate ravenously, using so much salt it was a wonder it didn't spoil the food. He ate, too, but not as much as he normally would. He was still half full from that steak.

As they ate, the window turned gray and the kitchen darkened. At one point he rose and lit the lamp.

"I should share this salt with some of the others," Melissa commented as she forked her last piece of egg. "Families I know, with children."

"It's yours to do with as you please."

She dabbed at her lips with a napkin. "What would please me now is to have dessert."

"I didn't make any," Fargo said.

Melissa smiled and looked him right in the eyes. "I wasn't referring to food."

# 12

Her brazenness surprised him.

Melissa came around the table, took him by the hand, and led him along the hall to her bedroom. Her hooded eyes never left his face. Once in her bedroom, she closed the door, pressed against him, and placed her hands on his shoulders. "You're being awful quiet."

"Wonder why," Fargo said, molding his hands to her bottom. He liked the feel of her breasts on his chest and the warmth of her thighs on his groin.

"I'm not being too forward, am I?"

"This will be one of the best desserts I've ever had," Fargo said, grinning.

"You don't know that. I'm afraid I don't have a lot of experience. To be frank, I've never wanted a man before as much as I want you."

"You're feeling better?"

"I feel fine, thanks to you." She kissed him, lightly at first but with increasing ardor.

Fargo let her set the pace. He could tell she was nervous and trying not to show it. He didn't suck on her tongue until her third kiss. Or cup a breast until the fourth. At the contact of his hand, she moaned deep in her throat and ground her hips.

Inwardly, Fargo smiled. There was no need to hold back anymore. He covered both her breasts and squeezed.

"Yessss. I like that," she cooed, digging her fingernails into him.

There was a lot Fargo liked. Such as running a hand down over her belly to her legs and stroking first one thigh and then the other. Her breath became as hot as the stove, and she lavished kisses on his face and neck.

It was a while before he steered her to the bed. She stretched out and lay on her back, a leg crooked invitingly, carnal desire in her eyes. "Like what you see?" she said when he stood there admiring her.

"You have no idea."

Fargo took off his gun belt and shed his spurs and his boots. As he crawled on beside her, she removed his hat and dropped it to the floor.

"We won't be needing that."

"And you won't be needing this," Fargo said as he pried at the first of the small buttons on her dress.

"Why do I have the feeling you've done this a lot of times before?" she playfully asked.

"Once or twice."

"You'll be gentle, won't you?"

"Except when you don't want me to."

"How will you know that?"

"I'll know."

They stripped naked and lay not quite touching, Melissa's eyes were wide with trepidation. Fargo went slow so as not to unnerve her. He kissed her face, her mouth, her neck. He rubbed her arms, her hips, her legs. As she warmed and responded with growing need, he turned his attention to her breasts. Inhaling a nipple, he sucked and tweaked it.

Melissa responded by gasping and pressing on the back of his head. "Yes," she breathed. "Oh, please, yes."

Her thighs were exquisite. Long and smooth and velvet soft.

She pleased him mightily by unexpectedly touching him, and running her hand along his full length.

"Goodness gracious," she gasped. "You're so big."

Fargo lathered and nipped until her chest heaved and she was tugging at his hair as if to pull it out by the roots.

The time came. He slid a hand to her wet slit. She stiffened at the contact but relaxed when he slowly stroked her. He took his time. They had all night. When he inserted a finger, she arched her body and her mouth parted in a soundless cry of pleasure.

More caressing incited her to a fever pitch. She cooed and rubbed excitedly against him.

When Fargo positioned himself on his knees between her legs, she gazed deep into his eyes and huskily said, "Ravish me."

Thrusting up into her, Fargo held himself still while she panted and raked his back and wrapped her legs around his waist. Commencing to ram into her, he stroked ever faster, ever harder.

Under them, the bed bounced and creaked.

Melissa groaned and tossed her head from side to side and exploded. "Yes!" she cried. "Oh, yes!"

Fargo felt her sheath contract, felt the ripples of delight that coursed through her.

He held off as long as he could, but there came that inevitable moment when his own body wouldn't be denied. "My turn," he said, and let himself go.

Afterward, they lay breathing heavily, Fargo's arm around her shoulders and her cheek on his chest.

"That was wonderful," she said sleepily.

Fargo grunted.

"We should do it again sometime."

Fargo couldn't agree more. For now, he closed his eyes and let himself drift off. He had a long day ahead tomorrow. The ride to the salt lick, spying for the town. He'd better keep his wits about him or he wouldn't make it back.

"Nothing to say?" Melissa asked.

"In an hour I'll be raring to go again."

"Promises, promises," Melissa teased. "You'll have to prove that, handsome."

Fargo did.

# 13

The lawman and the banker and the mayor, as well as several others, came to see him off at dawn.

"We wanted to show our support," one remarked. "You're risking your life on our account, after all."

The Ovaro stood saddled and ready in the growing shadow of the stable as a golden arch blazed the eastern horizon.

Melissa was there, too, a shawl over her shoulders, a rosy tint to her cheeks. "Please don't let any harm befall you. We could never forgive ourselves if it did."

Parkinson smirked and said, "While we appreciate his courage, let's not forget we're paying him two hundred dollars."

Melissa turned to the banker. "You might show a little more courtesy."

"What do you want me to do?" Parkinson asked. "Get down on my knees and praise him to high heaven?"

"Now, now," Marshal Bubaker intervened, "let's not bicker. We don't want to offend him. We have too much at stake."

"Are you offended, Mr. Fargo?" Parkinson sarcastically asked.

"Only by jackasses," Fargo said.

The banker turned red.

Gripping the saddle horn, Fargo swung on. He had a full canteen and a bundle of food, courtesy of Melissa. As he reined around, Marshal Bubaker stepped up.

"I've been asking around about that gent in the bowler you keep running into. A few people recollect seeing him. I checked at the boardinghouse, but he's not staying there. So either he has someplace to lie low or he camps outside of town at night."

"He's not from here?"

"Of that I'm sure. My guess is he works for Crillian and dresses like he does to blend in better."

"Or perhaps he's not connected to Crillian at all," Parkinson said. "Perhaps he has a grudge against our intrepid scout."

"I've never set eyes on him before," Fargo said.

"So you say."

"Keep it up." Fargo wondered why the banker was acting so unfriendly all of a sudden, and he wasn't the only one.

"Why are you picking on him?" Melissa asked.

"Don't be silly, my dear. I support his efforts on our behalf as fully as you do," Parkinson said. "Not that I would open my home to him," he added sourly.

"Enough," Marshal Bubaker said.

"Yes," Melissa said resentfully. "More than enough."

Parkinson shrugged. "It's your reputation."

"I mean it," Bubaker said.

Fargo touched his hat brim to Melissa and got out of there. Word had spread, and dozens of people watched him from windows or stepped out in their robes to watch him go.

Every last one had the by-now-familiar haggard look.

When Fargo reached the end of Main Street and looked back, Melissa and Bubaker and the banker were still bickering.

"Be glad you're a horse," Fargo said to the Ovaro.

The morning was cool but that wouldn't last long. Once the sun rose, he'd be sweltering.

Fargo rode at a walk. Sand and packed earth spread before him, with not a single plant anywhere.

Dunes appeared, a few bordering the road.

Fargo had gone past several and was coming up on one at the road's edge when a small figure in a suit stepped out with a six-shooter leveled. Fargo drew rein. "You again."

*"Bonjour,"* the small man said. "Have you missed me?"

"Not for a minute," Fargo said, annoyed at himself for being caught with his guard down. He hadn't expected trouble so close to town.

The man touched his hair. "I owe you for a hat. I saw you stomp on mine. Such a temper you have."

"How about I buy you a new one and we call it even?"

The small man grinned. "I'm afraid not. You will climb down, slowly, and hold your arms out where I can see your hands. Try to ride off and I'll shoot. Try any tricks at all and I'll shoot."

Fargo debated with himself. He was quick, but not quick enough to clear leather before the small man put lead into him. "What's your handle?"

"What do you care?"

"I don't. What is it?"

"I'm called Jaffer. Now, off your horse, *s'il vous plaît*."

Fargo dismounted with the speed of a turtle. Spreading his arms, he said, "How's this?"

"It's a start." Jaffer came closer. "Shed your gun belt. Let it fall. Use one hand and one hand only."

"Yes, Mother." Fargo pried at the buckle until it loosened and the belt and holster plopped to the earth at his feet. "Anything else?"

Jaffer put two fingers in his mouth and whistled.

Around the dune came a zebra dun, the reins wrapped around the saddle horn. It stopped next to Jaffer and bobbed its head.

"Nice animal," Fargo complimented him.

"I think so," Jaffer said.

Fargo glanced down. His holster had come to rest on his left boot. Most of the belt lay in the dust. "So now what? You take me to Crillian?"

"It amuses me that you think I work for him."

"Then who?" Fargo said in surprise.

"That is for me to know," Jaffer replied. "Trust me when I say it's the last thing you should be worried about." He paused. "Were I you, I'd be more concerned about how I will live out the day."

# 14

In his wide wanderings Fargo had learned a few things. One was that some badmen loved to hear themselves talk and would crow when they got the better of someone. Jaffer struck him as a crower.

"Didn't you hear me? I said by tonight you'll be dead."

"You're lying about not working for Crillian. No one else has any reason to want me dead."

"It is not that so much as to prevent you from making a mess of things."

"What the hell does that mean?" Fargo testily asked.

Jaffer changed the subject. "Tell me about Mademoiselle Gebhart. I know you spent the night at her house. Don't deny it. And don't deny what you did with her, either."

"Her curtains were closed."

"You and her under the same roof. What else would you do?"

"I never poke and tell," Fargo said.

"That's all right. The man I work for has no interest in her anymore."

"Is he somebody I know?"

"Nice try, *monsieur*," Jaffer said.

"You're French now?"

"I am many things. Mostly I solve problems for those who can afford to hire me. My standard fee is five hundred dollars."

Fargo whistled.

"Unfortunately for you, you have become a problem. You have stuck your nose in where you shouldn't."

"Then you're really not working for Crillian?"

"How many times must I say it? In English, no. In French, *non*. In fact, another reason my employer hired me is to see that Crillian doesn't do him harm."

"This is getting complicated," Fargo said.

"If you only knew," Jaffer replied.

"That's all you're going to tell me?"

"I have already said too much, perhaps. My employer does not want anyone to know he hired me. Yet another reason I must dispose of you."

"About that," Fargo said. Sweeping his leg up, he sent his gun belt flying at Jaffer's face even as he shifted to one side. Jaffer's six-gun went off, the slug missing Fargo's ear by a whisker. His holster caught Jaffer on the cheek, and Jaffer grabbed at it and swore.

Fargo sprang. Jaffer's revolver went off again but the lead went wide. Fargo grabbed hold of the smaller man's forearms and twisted to keep Jaffer from firing a third time. "Got you," he said. "Drop your smoke wagon."

Jaffer was strangely calm. He didn't try to break free. Instead he smiled and said, "If you think you've caught me, you have another think coming." And with that, he hopped into the air and kicked.

Fargo's jaw burst with pain. He tried to hold on but Jaffer tore an arm free—not his gun hand—and drove his fist into Fargo's gut. More pain exploded. Jaffer was small but he was solid muscle. Fargo rammed his knee at Jaffer's head, only to have Jaffer easily sidestep and retaliate with another kick.

Wrenching Jaffer's wrist, Fargo forced him to let go of the revolver. Jaffer didn't seem to care; he leaped into the air again and kicked at Fargo's throat. To protect himself, Fargo had to let go. He backpedaled, and the small man came at him with a vengeance.

"I don't need a gun to beat you."

"I'm trembling in my boots," Fargo said. He was a good two feet taller and outweighed Jaffer by sixty to seventy pounds.

"You will be."

Like a human rabbit, Jaffer bounded high and flicked a leg out. Fargo blocked it, but as Jaffer started to drop he spun in midair and kicked with his other boot, straight at Fargo's solar plexus.

Fargo doubled over. Retreating, he took deep breaths to try to steady himself.

Smiling smugly, Jaffer taunted, "I'm going to take my time with you, big man. Stomp you like you did my bowler." He dropped into a peculiar crouch. "Ever been to France, *vous grand boeuf*?"

"What?" Fargo said, struggling to straighten. "No."

"I have," Jaffer said, and launched himself like an arrow.

Fargo didn't know what France had to do with it. He got his arms up but the force of the kick still drove him back.

Landing lightly, Jaffer laughed. "Look at you. We've hardly begun and you're half-beaten."

"Go to hell, you damn runt."

"You first," Jaffer said.

Fargo blocked a kick to his face. Jaffer went at his knees and his groin, and the blows were harder to ward off.

It was like fighting a jackrabbit. Jaffer was always in motion, always jumping and bounding and spinning, and always kicking, kicking, kicking. He hardly ever used his hands. It was a form of fighting Fargo had never encountered, and the little man was extremely proficient at it.

Jaffer knew he was, too. He smirked the whole time and gave Fargo smug looks whenever Fargo swung and missed.

The hell of it was, slowly but inevitably Fargo was being worn down. He had more stamina than most, but he couldn't sustain the pace of their fight forever. And the little man seemed tireless.

Then Jaffer vaulted high and tried another kick at Fargo's throat. Fargo countered with his forearm. Once again, in midair, Jaffer performed one of those flashing spin kicks of his. Before Fargo could help himself, he was down, pitching to his hands and knees.

"Got you now," Jaffer crowed.

Fargo avoided a kick to his face by throwing himself to one side and rolling. Shoving into a crouch, he raised his fists.

Jaffer didn't attack. Instead he said, "I was born in New Orleans, but I spent a few years in Marseilles."

"Good for you."

*"Vous êtes stupide, grand homme."*

"I don't speak the lingo," Fargo said, thankful for the respite. The pain was lessening.

"Big men like you are always so stupid," Jaffer said.

"I haven't noticed an excess of brains in little ones," Fargo said.

"I won't lose my temper, if that's what you are trying to do."

"I bet you've hated big men all your life." Fargo sought to keep him talking.

"Why shouldn't I?" Jaffer retorted. "When I was little, bigger boys made my life a living hell. They were always mocking me, always picking fights. When I grew up it was the same. Stupid oxen like you who think they can get the better of me just because I had the misfortunate of being born small."

"Women must laugh themselves silly when you take off your britches."

Jaffer's face hardened. "I take back what I said about not losing my temper. For that remark, you will die a slow death."

"Big talk, little man," Fargo said.

"You asked for it," Jaffer said, and swept in anew.

# 15

Fargo was ready. When he'd rolled to his feet a minute ago, he'd scooped dirt into both hands as he rose. Now, as Jaffer executed another of those high kicks of his, Fargo threw the dirt in his left hand into Jaffer's eyes.

Jaffer performed a remarkable backflip and landed out of reach. Blinking furiously, he wiped at his face.

Darting in, Fargo slammed a fist to Jaffer's chest. Jaffer went down hard but was instantly up again, cursing and backing away. Tears streamed from his eyes. "That was a dirty trick."

"You expect me to fight fair when you're out to kick me to death?"

"I have a sense of honor. Which is more than I can say about you."

"*Honor*, my ass," Fargo said. "Women and kids are slowly dying and you're helping it happen."

"I do no such thing," Jaffer said. "I protect my employer's interests, nothing more. The women and children are none of my concern."

"We call that nitpicking," Fargo said.

"All the town has to do is pay Crillian what he asks and they can have all the salt they want."

"He's trying to break them and you know it."

"There is more to it than that, monsieur. Much more. But enough talk. Let us end this." Jaffer skipped at Fargo and cocked his leg for a kick.

Fargo threw the dirt in his right hand at Jaffer's eyes. This time Jaffer got both hands up to protect them, but, in doing so, left his body open. Fargo rammed a fist into Jaffer's gut, into his ribs, into his groin, all so fast that Jaffer had no chance to defend himself. Jaffer collapsed and writhed.

Fargo reclaimed his gun belt. Drawing his Colt, he stood over Jaffer just as Jaffer looked up. "I should just shoot you," he said, and clubbed Jaffer over the head.

Jaffer slumped, unconscious.

Bending, Fargo patted him down. He found the derringer up the little man's left sleeve. He stuck it, and Jaffer's six-shooter, into his own saddlebags. Then he took hold of the bridle to the zebra dun, turned the dun toward Inferno, and gave it a smack on the rump.

The horse trotted off.

Climbing on the Ovaro, Fargo resumed his ride. He looked back only once. Jaffer wasn't moving. "Damn runt," he muttered.

The temperature climbed.

Fargo was sweltering when bumps appeared in the distance. They slowly grew into the hills where he'd find the salt lick.

Fargo left the road and circled to come at the lick from a direction no one was likely to expect. Or so he hoped. Ignatius Crillian supposedly had close to twenty gun hands working for him. A worrisome number.

The last stretch to the hills was flat ground with no cover. If there were lookouts, they'd spot him.

As much as he didn't want to, Fargo brought the Ovaro to a gallop. Only when nothing happened and he drew rein in the shadow of the first hill did he breathe a little easier.

A gully was handy for hiding the stallion.

The Henry in hand, Fargo advanced on foot.

The hills were bare of vegetation. Boulders were scattered here and there, about the only cover to be had.

Fargo spied smoke. When he heard voices, he climbed to the crest of the next hill and flattened. Removing his hat, he peered over. He'd found the salt lick, over an acre in extent, the salt gleaming white in the burning sun.

An old cabin stood nearby, smoke rising from the chimney. Just beyond the cabin a long lean-to had been erected, and bedrolls and men were under it. It offered shade, if nothing else.

Horses were tied in a string, some with saddles, some without.

No one was working at the lick. A flatbed wagon without a team stood idle, and tools, mainly picks and shovels, were scattered about.

The men under the lean-to were loafing. They talked. They played cards. One was cleaning a rifle.

Fargo recognized two of them: Willy and Clell. He was debating whether to try to sneak closer when the cabin door opened and out came four men. Three he pegged from their descriptions.

A big man with short blond hair and oversized fists had to be

Werner, the German. He walked with a swagger, his fists always clenched.

A slender panther in a sombrero, a custom belt fitted with knives, and a revolver around his waist, must be Ramirez.

A third gent wore a pair of pearl-handled Remingtons, each rigged for a cross-draw. A flat-crowned black hat was pulled low over his face.

That left the fourth man.

"Ignatius Crillian," Fargo guessed.

The cause of Inferno's suffering wasn't very imposing. Not much over five feet, Crillian wore a suit and a derby and had a moon face. His jacket was open, and a Starr revolver was tucked under his belt. He walked over to the lean-to and addressed the men there, and presently two of them climbed on saddled mounts and rode off.

Based on what Fargo had seen so far, it shouldn't be hard for the townsfolk to move in under the cover of darkness, surround the place, and get the drop on Crillian's outfit. If the gun hands made a fight of it, though, the townsfolk were in trouble.

Movement brought Fargo out of his musing.

Two men with rifles were coming around the lick. They didn't act as if they knew he was there. Evidently Crillian sent men out every so often to scour the hills as a precaution.

Sliding down, Fargo donned his hat and hurriedly descended. He bore north, around the next hill. The men with the rifles were to the south, and taking their sweet time.

Fargo wanted to get close enough to eavesdrop. It was a gamble, but he might overhear something the townspeople could use to their advantage.

Boulders enabled him to reach a spot a stone's throw from the back of the cabin. The wall was windowless, which was good. Not so good was the outhouse, which stank to high heaven.

No sooner did Fargo hunker behind the last boulder than the outhouse door creaked and out shuffled a gun hand with his gun belt over his shoulder. He went around the far side.

If Fargo could reach the cabin undetected, he'd be close enough to the lean-to to hear whatever Crillian and the others were saying. Keeping low, he sprinted to the rear wall and flattened.

So far, so good. Fargo crawled to the corner. He could see into the lean-to—and Crillian wasn't there. Raising his head, he looked toward the horse string. Crillian wasn't there, either.

It might be that Crillian had gone back into the cabin, Fargo reckoned. He inched forward and glanced up. There was no window on that side, either. He decided to get out of there while his luck was still holding.

From behind him came the unmistakable clicks of gun hammers.

"How do you do, señor?" a voice said. "I would not move if I were you, or you will be very dead, very quick."

# 16

Fargo didn't move.

Boots crunched the ground and huge hands relieved him of the Henry and the Colt. The boots moved back.

"You may sit up if you like, señor."

"Slow as molasses," warned another voice, like flint.

Fargo had a good idea who had caught him.

The Mexican was relaxed and smiling, his slender hands on two of his knives. He was amused more than anything. Most would call him handsome. "Surprised, eh?"

"Am I ever," Fargo said.

"I am Ramirez. These are my amigos."

It was the big German who had relieved Fargo of his hardware. Werner had a jaw that jutted like an anvil, and the dull expression of an ox. "You're not too smart, mister, trying to sneak up on us."

"Ain't that the truth," said the flint-voiced man. His thumbs were hooked in his gun belt next to his pearl-handled Remingtons, and his eyes glittered with a hankering to use them.

"You must be Dreel," Fargo said.

Ramirez cocked his head. "You are well informed, señor. You're not here by accident, I think."

"Want me to knock him out?" Werner asked.

"What would be the use?" Ramirez said. "Señor Crillian will

want to talk to him. And besides, if he tries anything, Dreel will shoot him before he can blink."

Werner chuckled. "That he can."

"On your feet, señor," Ramirez said.

"Slow," Dreel said.

Fargo sighed. First Jaffer, now this. "It's not my day," he said, as he eased erect with his hands splayed. "How did you catch on to me, anyhow?"

Ramirez pointed at a hill to the south.

By squinting, Fargo made out a man near the top, seated on a boulder. "So there was a lookout."

"Did you think there wouldn't be?" Ramirez said, and grinned. "He saw you and waved his arms to get our attention and pointed. And here we are."

"Dumb of you," Werner said.

"Enough," Dreel snapped. "Let's take him to the boss."

Ramirez motioned. "After you, señor."

As they reached the front of the cabin, a shout at the lean-to brought the rest of the gun hands.

"Well, look who it is," Willy exclaimed.

Clell glowered and touched his bandaged shoulder. "I owe you, mister. And you're goin' to pay."

"This is the hombre who shot you and killed Nesbett and Timmy in town?" Werner said.

"The very same," Willy confirmed.

The cabin door opened and out strode Ignatius Crillian. He looked Fargo up and down and said, "Well done, gentlemen. Where did you find him?"

"Sneakin' up on us," Dreel said.

"He's not much good at it," Werner said.

"Oh, I expect he is," Crillian said. "He would have done just fine if not for the lack of cover." He held out his hand. "Ignatius Crillian. Although I'd imagine you already know that."

Surprised, Fargo shook.

"You haven't said who you are."

Fargo told him.

Crillian looked Fargo up and down a second time. "Are you the same Skye Fargo who took part in that marksmanship contest held in Missouri a while back? I read about it in the newspaper."

Fargo frowned. More people had heard about that than he could shake a stick at. "That was me," he admitted.

"Well, now, boys," Crillian said. "Be impressed. We are in the presence of someone who is halfway famous."
"Who?" Werner said.
Crillian nodded at Fargo. "This gentleman is reputed to be one of the best scouts alive. He also has a reputation for being as tough as they come."
"You don't say," Willy said.
"It explains a lot," Crillian said. "I no longer hold it against you, William, that he got the better of you. Twice."
"Thanks, boss," Willy said. "I told you he was mighty slick on the draw, remember?"
"Is he, now?" Dreel said. "Give him his pistol and let me try him."
"I'm afraid not," Crillian said.
"I can beat him," Dreel said. "I can beat anybody."
"Be that as it may," Crillian responded, "I must talk to him awhile. Then, perhaps, you can have him."
"I can't wait," Dreel said.
Fargo had run into men like Dreel before. Quick-trigger gents who thought they were God's gift to gun handling.
"Be careful what you wish for, Mr. Dreel," Crillian said. "But never you mind." He indicated the cabin door. "Señor Ramirez, would you and your friends escort our guest inside?"
*"Sí, señor."*
The interior was as much a surprise as Crillian. While the outside was rustic and plain, the inside boasted a rug on the floor, an oak table and chairs, and a small settee, of all things.
Crillian pointed at the table. "Why don't you have a seat, Mr. Fargo, and I'll make up my mind?"
"About what?" Fargo asked.
"Why, about whether you live or die, of course."

# 17

Fargo sat with his back to the fireplace, his hands folded on the table. He wanted to give the impression he wouldn't cause trouble.

Ramirez and the other two had spread out. Dreel was tapping his fingers on his gun belt. Werner still had the Henry and the Colt.

Ignatius Crillian pulled out a chair across from Fargo. "The place to begin, I suppose, is with who hired you to come to Inferno?"

"I'm only passing through," Fargo said.

Crillian shook his head. "I won't insult your intelligence if you don't insult mine. I'll ask you again. Who brought you here?"

"Until I ran into Willy and Clell, I had no idea this place existed."

Crillian frowned. "I was hoping we could be civilized about this." He turned toward the big German. "Werner, if you would be so kind."

Werner leaned the Henry against the fireplace and set the Colt on the floor beside it. Balling his enormous fists, he came toward Fargo with a smirk on his face. "I will bust your bones, little man."

"I need him able to talk," Crillian said. "Other than that, you're free to do as you please."

*"Danke,"* Werner said.

Dreel was poised to draw his six-shooters and Ramirez had two knives half out of their sheaths.

"You're making a mistake," Fargo said to Crillian.

"I'd like to believe you but I don't," Crillian said. "It's too much of a coincidence."

He stood and moved back. "Have at him, Mr. Werner."

The big German must have thought it would be easy, that Fargo wouldn't resist but would sit there and let himself be pummeled into the floor.

Fargo had other ideas. He waited for the moment when Werner rounded the table and came between him and Dreel. Heaving up, he rammed his fist at the big man's throat. He heard Ramirez shout something and a blade flashed past his face. His fist connected but didn't do more than make Werner blink. Before Ramirez could throw another knife, Fargo ducked under the table and skittered on all fours out the other side. He threw himself at an astonished Crillian even as one of Dreel's revolvers boomed and slivers flew from the top of the table. In a long bound he was behind Crillian with a forearm around Crillian's throat. Snatching the six-gun from under Crillian's belt, he jammed the muzzle against Crillian's temple and thumbed back the hammer.

The other three imitated stone: Ramirez with an arm hiked to throw another knife, Dreel with his six-shooters leveled, Werner looking confused.

"I'll blow his brains out," Fargo said.

"Dang, you're fast," Werner said. "You punch pretty good, too, mister. I almost felt that."

"Shut up, you simpleton," Dreel snapped.

Ignatius Crillian was oddly calm, as if having a gun to his head was the most ordinary thing in the world. "This was unexpected," he said. "It appears I've underestimated you. I won't make that mistake twice."

"Good for you." Fargo focused on Dreel and Ramirez. "Shed your weapons. Pronto."

Ramirez dropped the knife he was holding but Dreel hesitated, the muscles in his jaw twitching with fury.

"Even if you drop me, your boss is dead," Fargo said.

"Put down your *pistolas,* amigo," Ramirez urged. *"Por favor."*

"No one makes me drop my guns," Dreel growled.

"We owe it to Señor Crillian. He pays us well, does he not? I ask you again. For me, if not for the scout."

"Not even for you," Dreel said. In a blur, he suddenly twirled the revolvers into their holsters and jerked his hands in the air. "This is as far as I'll go, mister. If you don't like it, make your play."

Outside, shouts had erupted. Feet pounded and someone worked the front door latch.

"Stay out!" Crillian hollered. "Do you hear me?"

The latch stopped moving.

"What's goin' on in there, Mr. Crillian?" Willy wanted to know. "What was that shootin' about?"

"All of you are to go to the lean-to and stay there until I say otherwise," Crillian commanded.

"But, boss, what—?"

"Do as I tell you!" Crillian roared.

The hired guns moved away, grumbling.
Fargo nodded at the big German. "Bring my rifle and my six-gun over."
"Let go of Mr. Crillian first," Werner said.
"You don't have a say," Fargo said.
"Mr. Crillian," Werner said, "do I or don't I?"
"We must do as the scout wants for now," Crillian replied. "He momentarily has the upper hand."
"I don't like it none," Werner said, but he stepped to the fireplace and brought the Henry and the Colt over. "Here you go, mister."
Fargo grabbed his Colt. Cocking it, he gouged it against Crillian's head and tossed the other revolver to the floor. Taking the Henry, he motioned for Werner to move back. "Over where you were."
"Mr. Crillian?"
"Do it."
Reluctantly, Werner obeyed, saying, "If I ever get my hands on you, mister, I'll break your bones like they were twigs."
Fargo backed toward the front door, pulling Crillian after him. At the door he paused.
"Leave Señor Crillian and go," Ramirez said. "I give you my word we will not come after you."
"Speak for yourself," Dreel said.
Using two fingers of the same hand that held the Henry, Fargo cracked the door open far enough to see the lean-to. The gun hands were there, all right. But there was still the lookout on the hill and the pair patrolling the salt lick.
"What now?" Crillian said. "You have no hope of escaping. You know that, don't you?"
"You're going with me," Fargo informed him. "So long as you do as I say, I won't blow your brains out."
"No," Werner said.
"It's all right," Crillian told him. "Don't interfere. I'm perfectly safe so long as I don't lift a finger to try and stop him."
"If you say so, Mr. Crillian. But I don't like it none."
Shoving Crillian out ahead of him and keeping a firm grip on Crillian's shirt, Fargo hurried to the side of the cabin. The men at the lean-to spotted them and several started toward the cabin but stopped at a holler from Willy.
"What did you hope to prove by coming here, anyway?" Crillian asked. "Didn't anyone tell you how many men I have working for me?"

Fargo didn't answer. He saw no sign of the lookout and that worried him.

They reached the boulders, and Fargo moved faster. He intended to head for Inferno and take Crillian with him. He could collect the two hundred the town had promised and be on his way before sundown.

"There's a reason I was chosen for this task," Crillian said. "Would you care to hear what it is?"

"Someone *hired* you?" Fargo said in surprise. Here he'd thought Crillian had masterminded the whole scheme.

Crillian went to reply but a rifle lever rasped and someone called out, "Hold it right there, mister!"

# 18

It was the pair Fargo had seen circling the salt lick. They had made their circuit and were returning. Their rifles were raised but they didn't shoot. They didn't have a clear shot.

"Hold on, you two," Crillian said. "Don't do anything rash."

"Tell them to drop their rifles," Fargo said.

"You heard him," Crillian said. "You're to do as he says."

"But, boss—" one man said.

"I mean it, Harvey," Crillian said. "You do anything, anything at all, and I'm a dead man."

"I don't like it," Harvey said.

"Set your rifles on the ground this instant or you can look for work elsewhere," Crillian said. "I don't employ men who won't do as they're told."

The pair looked at each other. Harvey nodded and both lowered their rifles and stepped back with their arms in the air.

"Now your revolvers," Fargo said.

"Do it," Crillian said.

Fargo watched closely. They were itching to draw but they did as they were instructed. "Tell them to head for the lean-to."

Crillian did, and the pair began to move away.

Fargo turned Crillian, using him as a shield. For all he knew, one or both might have a derringer or some other hideout. He didn't move on until they had gone around the cabin.

"Well handled," Crillian said. "I thank you for not gunning them down."

"I should gun you."

"But you won't unless I resist," Crillian said smugly. "I've taken your measure, Mr. Fargo. You're not like Dreel. You don't kill for killing's sake."

They skirted the salt lick and were in among the hills. Wary of more lookouts, Fargo kept a sharp watch. He holstered the Colt and held the Henry with the muzzle against Crillian's back.

Crillian broke his silence with, "I have a proposal for you. How would you like to come and work for me?"

Fargo snorted.

"I'm serious. Why be enemies when there's no need to be? A man of your talents would be an asset."

"Listen to you," Fargo said.

"I'm no bumpkin, like Werner. You shouldn't make the mistake I did, and underestimate me."

"Hell, I don't know a damn thing about you," Fargo admitted, "or why you're trying to break the town."

"You don't have all the facts, I'm afraid. I, personally, am not trying to break anyone."

"Could have fooled me."

"If it's true you're only passing through, which I still doubt, mind you," Crillian said, "then you've become caught up in something that doesn't concern you. You should have simply ridden on."

"Your boy Clell tried to gun me."

"Is that what this is? You're getting back at me for what he did? If you don't mind my saying so, that's rather childish."

"You need more reasons? How about those two who tried to put windows in my skull in Inferno?"

"They overstepped themselves. Willy explained what occurred, and I regret their stupidity. Usually those who work for me do as I've told them." Crillian paused. "Which reminds me. You haven't said whether you'll take me up on my offer and come work for me?"

"No."

"Might I ask why?"

"The kids in Inferno."

"What are they to you? Do you know some of them personally?"

"No," Fargo said. "They're just kids. And because of you and whoever hired you, they're hurting."

"I'll be damned. Based on the stories I've heard, I'd assumed you were as hard as nails. But now I see that everyone is mistaken. You actually care."

"Go to hell."

"If you won't come work for me, I have another proposal. Let me go, here and now, and I give you my word that you can leave unmolested."

"I'm leaving anyway," Fargo said. He didn't mention that he was taking Crillian with him.

"It's in your own best interests. My men won't rest until they've buried you. Do you really want that?"

"I want you to stop talking."

"I'm not much of a fighter, myself." Crillian ignored him. "But I am a master strategist. It's why I was picked to oversee this operation."

"You're fond of yourself, I'll say that."

"My brain is my stock-in-trade, you might say," Crillian said. "Where men like Dreel rely on their quickness with Colts, I rely on the sharpness of my thinking."

"I bet you can listen to yourself all day."

Crillian chuckled. "Brilliance is, by its very nature, obvious to even the most common dullard."

"Ah," Fargo said, craning his neck for a glimpse of the stallion.

"Ah what?"

"You're one of those."

"It would be foolish of me to belittle my own abilities, would it not? I am a man of very special talents."

"Do you walk on water too?"

"You're not taking this seriously enough. But very well. Have your fun while you can. In a very short while it will come to an end."

# 19

Fargo spied the stallion, standing where he had left it, and gave Crillian a push to hurry him along.

Crillian stumbled and almost fell. "Must you be so rough? I'm doing as you demand, aren't I?"

"You bitch too much," Fargo said.

"I have a gun against my back. Excuse me for being irritable."

The Ovaro had raised its head and pricked its ears and was staring intently at them.

"The people of Inferno are going to be happy to get their hands on you," Fargo predicted.

"It wouldn't help them any."

"What's behind all this? Who hired you?"

"That's for me to know," Crillian said, "and for you to never find out."

The Ovaro, Fargo noticed, was still staring at them. He took a couple more steps, and then it hit him. The stallion was looking at something *behind* them. At the insight, he whirled.

A man Fargo had never set eyes on before was slinking toward them, probably intending to get as close as he could before shooting. The moment Fargo turned, the man whipped a rifle to his shoulder and fired. Fargo heard the buzz of lead past his ear as he raised the Henry and squeezed off a shot of his own. His aim was better. The man was jolted but gamely fired again. This time Fargo felt a prick at the whangs on his sleeve. Working the Henry's lever as fast as he could, he fired as the man went to shoot, fired as the man staggered, fired as the man fell to his knees and pitched forward.

Fargo had no time to congratulate himself. The back of his head exploded with pain, and the next he knew, he was on his own knees and was staring into the Henry's muzzle.

"You should have taken my offer," Ignatius Crillian said. At his feet lay a rock with a smear of blood.

Fargo boiled with anger—at himself.

"The tables have turned, have they not?" Crillian crowed. "A man of my intellect learns to adapt to every situation."

Fargo willed his vocal cords to work. "Don't you ever get tired of listening to yourself?"

"Your insults are becoming tiresome." Crillian stepped back. "Undo your gun belt and push it toward me."

"Damn me, anyhow," Fargo grumbled, his head pounding with the movement. He should have shot the son of a bitch when he'd had the chance.

"On your feet. You'll walk your animal to the cabin, and I will be right behind you."

Fargo put a hand to his head. There was a gash but it wasn't bleeding all that much. Snatching his hat off the ground, he slowly rose. A wave of dizziness caused him to sway.

"Take your time. I'm in no hurry," Crillian said gleefully.

Fargo shuffled to the stallion. His legs wouldn't work right and his head hurt worse.

"I hope I didn't hit you too hard. I wouldn't want you to die on me until I'm ready to have you killed."

"Bastard."

"Now, now. Pettiness ill becomes anyone."

"I ever get my guns back," Fargo said, "I'll show you petty."

"You were lucky the first time." Crillian grinned. "And I never make the same mistake twice."

Fargo wished he could say the same.

Crillian glanced over his shoulder and his grin widened. "Here come my associates to my rescue. Your fate, as they say, is sealed."

Ramirez, Dreel, and Werner, along with Willy and a dozen others, were coming around the last hill.

Willy waved and hollered, "Mr. Crillian! Here we are!"

"Isn't he adorable?" Crillian said, and laughed.

Fargo threw his hat at Crillian's face. It was only a hat, but Crillian reacted as most anyone would; he recoiled and raised the Henry to protect himself. Springing to the Ovaro, Fargo vaulted into the saddle. In another heartbeat he had reined around and resorted to his spurs.

Crillian yelled something and the Henry boomed just as Fargo bent over the saddle horn.

At a gallop, Fargo flew. He stayed low until he was well out of rifle range. The hired guns gave short chase but then stopped and stared after him. One raised a fist and shook it.

Fargo straightened. His head throbbed and the back of his neck was clammy from drying blood. Of more concern was the loss of his hat and the Henry and Colt.

He'd had them so long; they were as much a part of him as his skin.

Suddenly he remembered that Jaffer's six-shooter and the derringer were in his saddlebags. Drawing rein, he shifted around. The six-gun was a Colt, a standard production model with a longer barrel than his own and grips he didn't like, but it would do until he reclaimed his own. He shoved it into his holster. The derringer he left in his saddlebag.

His spirits improved slightly as he rode. His spying mission hadn't gone as well as he'd have liked, but he'd learned a few things that would aid the townsfolk if they attacked the salt lick.

Whether they did or they didn't was of no matter now. Because come what may, Fargo was going to repay Ignatius Crillian for that bash on the head. He was going to do what he should have done in the first place.

Fargo pointed his finger at the air and let down his thumb as if it were a gun hammer. "Bang," he said. "You're dead."

## 20

Twilight had fallen and windows glowed when Fargo rode into Inferno. His head had stopped throbbing but still ached. He went straight to the stable, and once the Ovaro had been stripped and watered and fed, made a beeline for the saloon. He bought a bottle, sat at the same corner table as before, and chugged.

Someone must have gotten word to Marshal Bubaker because not five minutes had passed when the batwings slammed open and in he rushed.

"You look like hell," were the first words out of his mouth.

Fargo grunted and pushed out a chair with his foot. "Have a seat. I'm not going anywhere for a while."

"Where's your hat?"

Instead of answering, Fargo downed more Monongahela. As he was wiping his mouth with his sleeve, in hurried the town banker, Parkinson.

"I sent for him," the lawman mentioned.

Fargo wasn't in the mood for small talk. The ride had baked him and, without his hat, the sun had about fried his brain.

"You're back!" Parkinson stated the obvious. "We were concerned it was taking you too long." He took a chair without being asked. "What did you learn? How many men does Crillian have? Can we overcome them with few casualties on our side?"

Fargo tilted the bottle once more.

"Why don't you answer me?" Parkinson asked. "Our welfare depends on what you've found out."

"Can't you see he's worn to a frazzle?" Marshal Bubaker said.

"All I see is him being contrary," Parkinson replied. To Fargo he said, "Don't sit there like a bump on a log. Too much is at stake. Should we or should we not attack the salt lick?"

"If you do," Fargo took pleasure in telling him, "you don't stand a snowball's chance in hell."

"Not even if we conscript every able-bodied man in town?"

"Conscript?" Bubaker said. "Doesn't that mean we'd force them? Like hell we will. Anyone who goes will go because they want to."

The batwings parted and in came Melissa Gebhart. Ignoring stares from some of the patrons, she hastened to their table. "I was told you were back," she said to Fargo. "You should have come see me."

"He's too busy drowning himself in liquor," Parkinson said. "Were I to guess, I'd say his vaunted nerve has been shattered."

Fargo set down the bottle and pointed at the banker. "Scat."

"I beg your pardon?"

"Make yourself scarce."

Parkinson sat up and thrust out his jaw. "Who do you think you are? You can't tell me what to do."

"I'll count to five," Fargo said, and commenced with, "One."

"Hold on," Marshal Bubaker said. "What are you up to?"

"Two," Fargo said.

"What will you do if I don't go?" Parkinson demanded.
"Three."
Parkinson turned to the lawman. "Are you just going to sit there or can I rely on you for protection?"
"Four."
"This is unheard of," Parkinson declared. Rising, he shoved his chair and it crashed to the floor. "I'll leave. But you have no cause for this barbaric behavior. No cause at all."
Fargo bent toward him. "Sure I do."
"What can it possibly be?"
"I don't like you."
Parkinson colored and harrumphed and turned on a heel. He was almost to the batwings when Mayor Hoffstedder entered. The banker grabbed him by the arm and hauled him out, the mayor feebly protesting.
"That was awful rude," Melissa remarked.
"He picked the wrong time to be an ass." Fargo treated himself to more Monongahela. He offered a taste to her and the marshal but both shook their heads. "Suit yourselves," he said, and swilled.
"Goodness," Melissa said.
Marshal Bubaker coughed. "If you're willing, I'd like to hear more about that snowball's chance we have."
"There are close to twenty of them," Fargo said.
"We already knew that."
"At least one is a top-notch gun hand and some of the others won't go down easy."
"We know that, too."
"They have lookouts and roving guards and the ground is so open, you can't get near them without them spotting you."
"Even at night, you reckon?"
"If you and your people can be as quiet as Apaches, you have a chance. If you can't—" Fargo didn't finish.
"Damn," Bubaker said, disheartened. "We have to do something. A little girl is so sick, she's liable to die at any time. There's no way for us to do it? No way at all?"
"I'll ponder on it," Fargo said. "After."
"After what?"
Fargo stood and walked around the table and clasped Melissa's wrist. "Let's go, gorgeous."
"Where are we going?"

Fargo stared.

"Oh," Melissa said, and colored redder than the banker. "You take a lot for granted, I'll have you know."

"Do I?" Fargo pulled and she willingly rose and followed. He held a batwing for her.

"Is it me or are you feeling randy?" Melissa said. "You could stand to relax a little."

Fargo admired her bosom and the sweep of her thighs, and grinned. "That's the plan, ma'am."

# 21

The same room, the same bed.

Fargo devoured her. They were no sooner inside than he grabbed her and pulled her close and sucked her tongue into his mouth. He cupped a breast and squeezed, and felt her nipple harden through the cotton.

Melissa groaned.

Fargo wasted no time in getting her on the bed. Scooping her into his arms, he carried her over and virtually threw her on it. Melissa gasped as he sprang on next to her and began to shed both their clothes. In his hunger he accidentally ripped off a button but she didn't complain.

Then they were naked, and Fargo went at her as if he hadn't been with a woman in ten years. He kissed and licked and bit and caressed, and she was panting huskily and quivering with her need.

"Do me," she pleaded.

Spreading her thighs, Fargo ran his member over her slit.

Melissa looked him in the eyes and dug her fingernails into his shoulders.

"What are you waiting for?"

Fargo answer was to ram up into her the full length of his pole.

Arching her back, Melissa parted her lips and let out a tiny mew that grew to a loud moan. She wrapped her legs tight around him and met his thrusts with pumps of her hips.

"Yes. Yes."

Fargo shut her up with another kiss. His body became a steam engine piston, stroking with smooth precision. He rammed in and out, in and out, the bed bouncing under them.

Melissa exploded first in a frenzy of release. When she realized he was still hard, and he resumed stroking, her eyes widened and she whispered, "You're magnificent."

Fargo needed this one. His close calls at the salt lick had left him tense and angry and this was the quickest way he knew to be his usual self. Liquor could do it but took a lot longer.

At length he crashed over the brink.

Melissa clung to him, weathering the storm of his violent desire. This time when he was done he coasted to a stop and collapsed on top of her. They both lay gasping for breath until he rolled off her onto his back.

"You wore me out," Melissa breathed. "No one has ever done that to me before."

"Give me ten minutes and I'll wear you out again."

Melissa giggled, thinking he was kidding.

Fargo was caked with sweat and his chest hammered, but he felt a lot less tense and his anger was mostly gone.

As if she were privy to his thoughts, Melissa remarked, "You made love as if you were mad at me."

"Not you."

"Then who?" Melissa asked.

"Myself, mostly," Fargo said. "And at Crillian and some of those who ride for him. I owe them, and it rankles."

"Owe them how?"

"They tried to kill me."

"Ah." Melissa rolled onto her side and placed her cheek on his chest. "That I can understand. But why be mad at yourself?"

"I was careless. I lost my hat, my rifle, my revolver."

"And you want them back?"

Fargo closed his eyes. He didn't want to think about it just then. He'd only become mad again.

"I'm only trying to understand," Melissa said. "There's more to you than meets the eye, I think."

"I'm a man," Fargo said.

"Not all men are alike. Some are less"—Melissa seemed to

search for the right word—"manly. Some are weak. Some are timid. You're neither."

Fargo grunted.

"You have a quality about you. A pureness I like and respect. It's a trait not a lot of men have."

"There's nothing pure about me," Fargo said.

"You misunderstand. By that I mean you don't whine and cry. You don't take guff. You don't let a woman make love to you. You make love to her. You're a man as men were meant to be."

"If you say so." Fargo wished she would hush. He could feel his anger rebuilding.

"I do," Melissa said. "I truly believe there are types of men, just as there are types of women. Some women, for instance, won't kiss a man below his waist. Other women will. That's what I mean by types."

Fargo stayed silent, hoping she would take the hint.

"Some people will only kiss on the lips. They never let anyone stick a tongue in their mouth. They think it's disgusting."

"Damn, woman," Fargo said.

"What is the matter? I'm only explaining how I feel. Sometimes after I've made love I like to talk. I can't say why. It just comes over me."

With an oath, Fargo opened his eyes and rolled on top of her.

"What are you doing?"

"Shutting you up," Fargo said, and squeezed a tit.

Melissa's eyes became hooded with lust. Grinning, she said, "I was hoping you would."

# 22

Fargo spent the night.

By the clock on her table, it was pushing eight when sounds roused Fargo into propping himself on his elbows. He heard the clang of a pan and humming. He also smelled food.

His stomach rumbling, Fargo rolled out of bed and dressed. He took his time. He had nowhere to be, nothing to do. His gun belt went on last. He took out the revolver he'd taken from Jaffer, and frowned. He wanted his own Colt. He'd been wrong; he did have something to do.

Melissa was bundled in a robe. She had two pans on the stove, bacon simmering in one, scrambled eggs in the other. At the moment she was spreading jam on pieces of toast. "You're up!" she exclaimed, and greeted him with a warm kiss. "Aren't you the sleepyhead?"

Fargo didn't bother telling her that he could count the number of times he'd slept past sunrise on his fingers and toes and have some left over. He pulled out a chair. "You cook, too?"

Melissa laughed. "I bake the best pies this side of anywhere. I sew and knit as well." She gave him a pointed look. "A man could do a lot worse."

"Don't go there," Fargo said. She would only be disappointed.

"I was only saying."

She whisked about, taking plates and cups and saucers from a cupboard and silverware from a drawer and setting them out, humming all the while.

Fargo didn't let her cheerfulness spoil his grumpy mood but he did put his hat and his guns from his mind for the time being. He owed her that. She'd been a voracious bed partner. If she ever took a husband, the man was in for nights that others would envy.

"A penny for your thoughts," Melissa said as she brought the coffeepot over to fill his cup.

"I was thinking about how I can't wait to meet up with

Crillian again," Fargo fibbed. She might make more of his thoughts about a husband than there was.

"From what you told me last night, you were lucky to make it out alive." Melissa poured and carried the pot to the stove. "Why push it?"

"I'm one of those manly men, remember?"

Melissa chortled. "You're not going to let me hear the end of that, are you? But it's true." She grew serious. "Just don't let it get you killed."

Fargo rarely used sugar but he did like cream and added some from a small china pot she had placed on the table.

Melissa was forking strips of bacon onto a plate. "By the way, we had a town meeting while you were gone yesterday."

This was news to Fargo. "Oh?"

"It was about you, and our attack on the salt lick."

About to take another swallow, Fargo stopped. "Oh?" he said again.

Melissa nodded. "The marshal went around telling everyone to meet at the saloon not long after you rode out."

"Tell me about it."

She brought the bacon over and set it down and returned to the stove for the scrambled eggs. "The mayor told how you were off at the salt lick spying on Crillian for us and—"

"Let me get this straight," Fargo broke in. "Hoffstedder told everybody in Inferno?"

"Yes. Why? What's wrong with that?"

"What else did the mayor say?"

"He had the marshal get up and explain how once you got back, we're attacking the salt lick. Nearly every man in town has volunteered to go. A lot of the older boys, too. And some of the women."

"Women?"

Melissa nodded. "The mayor said that women can shoot as good as men, so why not? I was one of those who stood up and told him I'd be happy to do my part."

"The women," Fargo said.

"What's gotten into you? Our lives are at stake. If we don't get salt, and soon, a lot of us will die. Women as well as men. Children, too." She brought the eggs over and handed him a large wooden spoon. "Help yourself and dig in. There's enough for seconds and thirds if you'd like."

Fargo was more interested in the meeting. He scooped some food, asking, "What else did they talk about?"

"Mainly the attack. There will be close to forty of us. We'll all have rifles and we'll go in quiet-like and catch Crillian and his gun hands when they're asleep." Melissa sat across from him. "We can end our suffering once and for all."

"This was the mayor's brainstorm?"

"Mr. Parkinson had a hand in it, I believe," Melissa replied. "Marshal Bubaker said he'd like to hear what you found out before he committed to an attack. I got the impression he wasn't fond of the idea."

"At least one of you has brains."

Melissa had taken a bite of toast, and stopped chewing. "We have to do *something*. Unless you have a better way to go about it, you shouldn't be so insulting."

They ate for a while in silence.

Fargo had thought the mayor and company were going to wait to hear from him before they made up their minds about an attack on the lick. Now everyone knew. It could be that word would reach Ignatius Crillian, and the townsfolk would ride right into an ambush.

"Without that salt, we won't make it to winter," Melissa commented. "You can see that, can't you?"

"Lead kills a lot quicker."

"You sound mad again. If you're against the idea, take it up with the mayor and Mr. Parkinson."

"I intend to," Fargo said.

# 23

Marshal Bubaker, Mayor Hoffstedder and the banker Parkinson made it easy for him. They were all at the saloon.

Fargo pulled out a chair without being asked, turned it around, and straddled it. "Gents," he said.

"We've been waiting for you to show up," Marshal Bubaker said.

Parkinson smirked. "I reasoned this was the one place you

were likely to come to when you were done with your visit to Miss Gebhart. Your fondness for liquor is no secret."

"Scandalous behavior," Mayor Hoffstedder muttered. "A proper lady wouldn't invite someone like you into her home and certainly wouldn't let him stay an entire night."

"Someone like me?" Fargo repeated.

Marshal Bubaker put a hand on the mayor's arm. "We're here to talk about Crillian and the salt lick. Nothing else."

"I agree with the mayor," Parkinson said. "Her behavior has been scandalous. When an opportunity arises, I intend to talk to her about it."

"No," Fargo said. "You won't."

"You don't live here," Parkinson said archly. "We're a small town. A small community. We can't have people flaunting their immorality. Gossip will spread. Miss Gebhart doesn't know it yet but she'll be regarded as a hussy."

Mayor Hoffstedder bobbed his chin. "People will look down on her. They'll whisper behind her back. No one will ever treat her the same again."

"No one is ever going to find out," Fargo said.

"You can't stop rumors from spreading," the mayor said.

"Sure I can," Fargo replied. "Only three people know I spent the night with her." He looked at each of them in turn. "The only way for gossip to start is for one of you to flap your gums."

"I'd never say a word to anyone," Marshal Bubaker said. "What Melissa does is no one's business but hers."

"I trust you to keep quiet," Fargo told him. "It's these other two bastards. One more than the other." He stared at Parkinson.

"How dare you," the banker said.

"I hear of any gossip," Fargo said, "or she gets word to me later that folks are whispering, I'll come back."

"Was that a threat?"

"A promise," Fargo said.

The banker started to stand but Marshal Bubaker gripped his wrist. "Hold on. This is getting out of hand. We're here to talk about Ignatius Crillian and the fact our town is being starved of salt when we need it most. Not to argue over Miss Gebhart."

"This scout puts on airs," Mayor Hoffstedder said. "I don't like it."

"You heard him threaten me," Parkinson said to the lawman, "yet you sit there and do nothing."

"I can't arrest a man for words," Marshal Bubaker said.

Fargo was fed up. He had half a mind to walk out. "I heard about the meeting you called."

"We've enlisted the help of every able-bodied man and some of the women," Hoffstedder said. "All we need is information from you on how to sneak in and take them by surprise."

"You can't."

"There has to be a way," Parkinson said. "It's why you went out there. To find one."

"I didn't. They have too many lookouts. And they might know by now what you have planned."

"How could they?" Hoffstedder scoffed.

"Unlike you," Parkinson said, "the citizens of our fair town have a sense of decorum."

"If that's your notion of an insult," Fargo said, "you need to work at it."

"God, I hate you," Parkinson said.

"Here we go again," Marshal Bubaker said, and sighed. "Forget about that. The important thing is the lick. We can't wait much longer. If we're going to drive Crillian and his men off, we have to do it before we're all too sick to lift a gun." He paused. "Fargo, be honest with me. Is it really as hopeless as you make it out to be?"

"It would be mice against cats," Fargo said, "and some of the cats are mountain lions."

"Ridiculous," Mayor Hoffstedder said. "We'll have thirty-nine guns. Twice the number they have."

"It's not the guns," Fargo said. "It's who is using them."

"Most of the men in town have shot a gun a few times," Hoffstedder said. "And we'll give lessons to those who haven't. It's simple, after all, to point and aim. I've done it myself and had no difficulty whatsoever."

"Did you hit what you were shooting at?" Fargo asked.

Hoffstedder shrugged. "I was ten or twelve, and my father had set up clay pots. No, I didn't hit them. But I distinctly recall he said that I only missed by a few inches. I would have shot more times but it hurt my shoulder. And it made my ears ring something terrible."

Fargo looked at the lawman. "Are you as stupid as they are?"

"They hired me. They pay me. I have to go along with whatever they want to do," Bubaker said.

"Even when it could get most of your town dead?"

"Even then."

"Can we count on your help or not?" Mayor Hoffstedder wanted to know.

Marshal Bubaker quickly said, "You've been out there. You know what to expect. With you along, we have a better chance."

"It's suicide," Fargo said.

"Please," Bubaker said. "This isn't your fight, and we hardly know each other. But I'm begging you, man to man."

"Hell," Fargo said.

# 24

At times Fargo couldn't believe how ridiculous folks could be. This was one of them.

Another meeting was held. Hoffstedder stood up and announced that the Inferno Army, as he called it, would head out at noon the next day and be in position to attack the salt lick by nightfall.

At the conclusion, the mayor asked if anyone had a comment.

"I do," Parkinson said, rising. "I've been giving our enterprise a lot of thought and I've come to agree with Mr. Fargo. We should rethink this. We're not soldiers. We're ordinary people. Most of us have never harmed a living soul. Crillian's pack of killers will eat us alive."

Fargo was genuinely surprised. He regarded the banker with a smidgen of newfound respect.

"You, of all people, are against it?" Hoffstedder said. "What other choice do we have?"

"We can pay the price Crillian demands," Parkinson said.

"For how long? Six months? Seven? By then our coffers will be empty and we'll have to go through this all over again."

"Better that than be slaughtered," Parkinson argued.

"I'll put it to a vote," Mayor Hoffstedder said. "But before I do, I have something to say." He gazed about the room. "Look around you. All of you. Look at the faces of your friends and acquaintances. Look at how sickly we all are. Think of the ones who aren't here because they are too sick to come. Think of the children who are too weak to get out of bed. Think of the cramps and the headaches and the seizures we suffer." He paused. "We need salt. We need it desperately. Granted, if we'd met Crillian's outrageous demands six months ago, we wouldn't be in the shape we are. But we didn't. We refused to let him extort money from us. Were we wrong? I don't think so. There's such a thing as dignity, and we refuse to compromise ours."

No one interrupted. They were hanging on every word.

"This may be our one and only chance to set things right. To ensure that we and our loved ones get the salt they need before it's too late."

Someone called out, "We're with you, Mayor!"

"It's natural if some of you have qualms," Hoffstedder continued. "Yes, we're stepping outside the bounds of the law. But we have that right. Our very lives are at stake. It's Crillian or us, and I, for one, will not let it be us."

Applause broke out.

"What do you say to that?" Hoffstedder asked the banker.

Parkinson frowned. "I still agree with Fargo. We're not gun hands. We outnumber them but they outgun us, as it were. Unless we take them by surprise, I'm concerned about the outcome."

"That's why Fargo has agreed to guide us," Hoffstedder said. "So we *do* take them by surprise."

Fargo felt compelled to say, "Don't count on that. I told you they have lookouts. And they patrol the lick."

"Evidently I have more faith in you than you do in yourself," Hoffstedder said.

The meeting was adjourned. Some of the townspeople drifted off but a lot stayed to talk.

Fargo rose to get out of there and a hand fell on his shoulder.

"You shouldn't look so glum," Melissa said. "It might turn out better than you expect."

"You're loco if you go."

"Inferno is my home. I have to help. For the sake of the children, if no other reason."

"None of you has any idea what you're letting yourselves in for," Fargo said.

"We have you to help us."

"Don't your ears work? If we go out there, a lot of you won't make it back."

"I agree with Hoffstedder. I have confidence in you."

"Damn it," Fargo said.

"By the day after tomorrow our nightmare will be over. We'll have control of the salt lick and everyone will be on the mend." Melissa lowered her voice, and grinned.

"How about coming over later?"

"Why wait?" Fargo said.

"I have a few people to talk to. You can go to my house. The door isn't locked." She touched his hand. "I won't be long."

Fargo saw Hoffstedder coming toward him and got out of there. He was mad enough to punch the fool. Once outside, he breathed deep of the cooler evening air and bent his boots to Melissa's. Another night of lovemaking appealed to him. A good breakfast in the morning, and he would lead them to their doom.

He supposed he could refuse to go along, but they'd likely try anyway and stand even less of a chance of surviving.

Melissa's house was dark. He went up the path to her small porch and opened the door. His spurs jangling, he walked down the hall to the kitchen and over to the drawers. The lucifers were in the middle one. He lit a lamp that hung on the wall, blew out the lucifer, and turned.

"Remember me?" Jaffer said. He was seated at the table. Somewhere he had gotten his hands on another revolver.

Fargo drew up short. The six-shooter was cocked and leveled at his belly. "I should have known I hadn't seen the last of you."

"You beat me," Jaffer said. "No one has ever done that before."

"A runt like you?"

Jaffer smiled. "When will you learn? I won't lose my temper and do something reckless." He tilted his head, studying Fargo quizzically. "I have a question for you."

"I was wondering why you didn't just shoot me."

"That's my question," Jaffer said. "Why didn't *you* shoot *me* out on the road? You could have killed me and didn't."

"You were out cold."

"That's your reason?" Jaffer chuckled. "*Un homme d'honneur*, eh? You have a sense of honor." He raised his revolver. "How unfortunate for you that I do not."

# 25

Neither of them had heard the front door open, but they both heard Melissa Gebhart call out, "Skye, are you back there?"

In a twinkling Jaffer was out of the chair and over by the stove where she couldn't see him. "Not a word," he said, putting a finger to his lips and menacingly extending his revolver.

Fargo tensed to spring. For all he knew, Jaffer would shoot her the moment she entered the kitchen.

As if sensing his thoughts, Jaffer said, "Don't worry, monsieur. I can't kill her. It is forbidden."

"Skye?" Melissa said from the hallway. "Why don't you answer me?"

Jaffer shook his head.

"Skye?"

Melissa appeared in the doorway, a smile on her face fading as she glanced from Fargo to Jaffer and back again.

"If you scream, mademoiselle," Jaffer said, "I will shoot him dead."

"Who are you?" Melissa demanded. "What are you doing here?"

"I am called Jaffer," the small man said with a courtly half bow. "As to the other, that should be apparent. Your friend and I have a matter that must be settled."

Melissa took a step. "I won't have this, you hear," she said angrily. "I want you out of my house this instant."

"I'm afraid that's not possible."

"Then you'll have to shoot me because I won't let you harm him. I'll scream and all the people out in the street will hear me and come running."

"In the street?" Jaffer said skeptically.

"We just had a town meeting. Everyone is heading home," Melissa said. "There are dozens out there right this minute."

From out in the street came the low babble of voices.

*"Merde,"* Jaffer said. "If it's not one thing, it's another." Cover-

ing Fargo, he sidled toward the back door. "You have more lives than a cat."

Fargo was dumfounded. The man had him dead to rights.

"I will spare you the sight of blood on your floor," Jaffer said to Melissa. "But the next time he and I meet, there will be a reckoning."

"Wait," Melissa said. "What is this about?"

"You already know," Jaffer said.

"The salt," Melissa said.

Jaffer reached the door and reached behind him and worked the latch. "No, mademoiselle. The salt is a factor but the true cause is that people do not listen."

"Don't you care that women and children are suffering because of that awful man?"

About to slip out, Jaffer said, "To which awful man do you refer?"

"Ignatius Crillian, of course."

"You mix apples and oranges, as they say." Jaffer gave another bow and darted out, pulling the door shut after him.

"What are you waiting for?" Melissa asked when Fargo just stood there. "Aren't you going to go after him?"

"No."

"Why in heaven's name not?"

"He said he wouldn't bloody your floor. He didn't say he wouldn't bloody your grass." Besides which, Fargo would be a perfect target as he went out the door.

"How did he know you would be here?"

"He's been spying on me," Fargo said. He walked over and looped an arm around her waist. "How about if we take up where we left off last night?"

"Hold on," Melissa said, pushing away. "What's to stop that little man from sneaking back in here in the middle of the night and killing you?"

"Nothing," Fargo had to admit.

"Well then. Wouldn't it be wiser for you to keep your clothes on and keep an eye on things?"

"I can keep my clothes on and still do it."

Melissa stared at the back door and gnawed her lip. "No," she said. "I'd be worried the whole time. It wouldn't be any fun for me."

Fargo tried to persuade her but it was a lost cause. Eventually she turned in. He extinguished the lamp and sat at the kitchen table drinking coffee from a fresh pot she had brewed.

He had a lot to ponder, not the least of which was how to keep the good people of Inferno from getting themselves killed. The only real advantage they'd had was the element of surprise, and that might have been lost.

The best he could do, Fargo reckoned, was to lead them to the north of the salt lick. Crillian would expect them to come from the south, and the road. The problem with that was the lookouts.

Another idea was to lure the gun hands out into an ambush. But how? Fargo asked himself. Crillian and Ramirez and Dreel weren't idiots. They'd smell a trap, and it would be all over for the townsfolk.

He emptied his cup and poured another. He was restless. Cup in hand, he prowled the house, going from window to window and peering out without showing himself.

Not a solitary light glowed anywhere.

He peeked in on Melissa. She was curled on her side, her head deep in her pillow, snoring lightly.

Refilling his cup yet again, Fargo made himself comfortable on the settee in the parlor. He ran a hand through his hair, wishing he had his hat. He felt undressed without it. The same with his own Colt.

He must have been sitting there an hour when a strange sound perked his ears. It came from the front door, a *scritch-scritch-scritch* as of something scratching.

Instantly on his feet, Fargo drew the six-shooter. He crept to the door and put an ear to it. The scratching had stopped. He listened and, when nothing happened, was about to turn and go back when he heard a meow. Melissa hadn't said anything to him about having a cat, but then, why should she? They'd had other things on their minds.

He supposed if he didn't let it in, it would keep scratching and meowing. Working the bolt, he opened the door.

"Don't you feel stupid?" Dreel said. He was standing back out of reach, a pearl-handled Remington in each hand.

Ramirez was leaning against the jamb, skillfully flicking a knife from finger to finger. "Don't feel bad, amigo," he said, and scraped the tip on the door. "I do a good cat." He grinned and said, "Meow."

# 26

Fargo didn't stand a prayer if he drew. Either Dreel would shoot him or Ramirez would bury a blade in him, or both.

"Step outside, *por favor*," Ramirez said. "We wouldn't want to wake the señorita, yes?"

Fargo did as they wanted. He wouldn't risk harm befalling Melissa. "This isn't my night. First the runt. Now you two."

"By runt you must mean Señor Jaffer," Ramirez said, quietly closing the door. "And there are more than two of us, señor."

Werner's huge bulk materialized out of the gloom. So did the man everyone in Inferno hated.

"We meet again," Fargo said.

"Indeed we do," Ignatius Crillian said. "It must come as a considerable shock."

"This is the last place I expected you to turn up," Fargo confessed. "With everyone out for your hide."

"At this time of night they're all asleep," Crillian said. He looked at Werner and pointed at Fargo's holster and snapped his fingers.

"Yes, sir, Mr. Crillian," Werner said. He relieved Fargo of the revolver and stepped back.

"Let's get this hombre on a horse," Dreel said. "I won't rest easy until he's hogtied."

"It's unusual for you to have a case of nerves," Crillian said.

"Nerves, hell," Dreel growled. "He got away the last time. The boss will be mad if he does it again."

"Which boss would that be?" Fargo said.

"Tell him everything, why don't you?" Crillian snapped at Dreel, and then beckoned to Fargo. "You're coming with us. So long as you behave you won't be harmed. I would as soon kill you here and now but someone wants to talk to you."

Willy appeared, and a couple of other gun hands besides.

Fargo was ringed and led around to the side where another man waited with their mounts.

"We brought a horse just for you," Crillian said, indicating a sorrel.

"I'd rather ride my own."

"Your horse stays here. We want to leave a message." Crillian gestured. "Up you go."

"What kind of message can my horse be?" Fargo asked as he went to climb on. He wasn't about to try anything. Not with six pistols pointed at him.

"First we light a shuck," Crillian said.

At a loss, Fargo had to submit to being ushered in a wide loop that brought to them to the road out of town to the west.

Ignatius Crillian seemed to relax a little. Riding on Fargo's right, he remarked, "This should nip their grand plan in the bud."

"You've lost me," Fargo said.

"Isn't it obvious? The people of Inferno intend to attack us tomorrow. They're counting on you to lead them. It's not far-fetched to surmise that with you unable to, they'll change their minds." Crillian chuckled. "When they find that you're missing but your horse is still there, they'll rightly guess I had a hand in it. It should discourage them greatly."

"So that's what this is," Fargo said. "How did you find out about their plan?"

"That will be my little secret for the time being," Crillian said. "In a way, I've done them a favor by sparing their lives."

"You don't know them like I do," Fargo said. "They'll attack the lick with or without me."

"Let's hope not, for their sakes."

"What do you care if they live or die?"

"I don't. I'd just like to get this over with, with as few headaches as possible."

Crillian gazed at the stars, and smiled. "A fine night, don't you think? Although I would imagine your predicament prevents you from enjoying it."

"If you want their money so much," Fargo said, "why don't you rob the damn bank?"

"Now there's an idea, but, no, this isn't just about the money. This is about making those folks suffer."

"Your boss again," Fargo said.

"We were never trying to break them. From the start, they were supposed to suffer slowly, over a period of months."

"Some of them are kids."

"Is that a feeble attempt to touch my heartstrings?" Crillian said cheerfully. "I have news for you. I don't have a heart. It's why I was hired to ramrod this operation. I do what has to be done. No regrets, ever."

Fargo looked ahead. They were coming to a bend, with a low knoll to the right of the road.

"With you out of the way, they'll realize how futile it is to fight us," Crillian went on. "We'll give them even more incentive not to once the boss has talked to you."

Fargo firmed his grip on the reins.

"They need to see that there is no way out for them, save one. Or they'll wind up like you."

"Me?" Fargo shifted in the saddle, ready to use both legs at once.

"Ever hear of an object lesson? That's what you're going to be. Or part of you, anyhow."

"Part of me?" Fargo kept him talking. Another few yards and they would be at the knoll.

"Oh. That's right. I haven't told you yet." Crillian smirked. "We're fixing to chop off your head and leave it in the middle of Inferno's Main Street. That should get their attention, don't you think?"

Fargo used his spurs.

## 27

With a jab of both heels, Fargo reined to the right. The startled sorrel slammed into Willy's mount and Willy bleated and hauled on his own reins. Another jab, and Fargo was past him and racing around the knoll. He braced for the blast of shots but there weren't any.

"After him!" Ignatius Crillian bawled. "And remember, we want him alive!"

Fargo had no time to wonder why. Lashing the reins, he flew as fast as the sorrel could go. It wasn't the Ovaro. Some horses were faster than others and this one wasn't molasses but it wasn't chained lightning, either.

Behind him hooves thundered.

"This way!" someone shouted. It sounded like Werner.

The terrain was mostly flat and open but there was no moon. Fargo was confident he could slip away if he could put distance between them.

The thunder grew louder.

For long minutes the chase continued. To Fargo's consternation, the sorrel showed signs of flagging. Desperate, he glanced right and left. There was no cover to be had.

A gambit occurred to him. It might get him killed but it was his only hope. He used his spurs again, lashed the reins, and the sorrel tapped whatever reserves of stamina it had and galloped faster.

Fargo looked back. Two or three were maybe forty yards behind him. It was hard to judge.

Sliding his boots free of the stirrups, Fargo slid onto the side of the saddle, hanging one-legged, Comanche fashion. He only hung for a few moments. With a push, he was clear and falling. He hit hard on his shoulder, rolled, and flattened on his belly with his arms over his head for protection. He prayed the sorrel kept galloping. If it stopped, he was in trouble.

The sorrel didn't stop.

Then the thunder was right on top of him, filling his ears and shaking the ground as darkling riders swept by. Hooves thudded mere feet from where he lay.

The rest were close behind.

Fargo lay there, braced for the heavy impact of a hoof and the crunch of his bones. But the gun sharks swept on.

Rising, Fargo turned to the east and ran. He needed to put as much ground between them as he could before they discovered the sorrel was riderless.

His shoulder was throbbing but he didn't let it slow him. He ran as if a horde of Apaches were on his heels, ran until his chest was heaving and his legs were quaking and he couldn't run another step if he wanted to.

Stopping, Fargo bent over with his hands on his knees, sucking in air. He listened but couldn't hear anything over his own breathing. Much too slowly, he recovered enough that he heard the thump of a hoof. He dropped flat and lay still, hoping he hadn't been spotted.

It was a single rider, approaching at a walk in a sort of S pattern, carefully searching. Apparently the gun hands had spread out to hunt him down.

Fargo slid his knee toward his chest, hiked his pant leg, and palmed the Arkansas toothpick.

A silhouette of the horse and rider appeared. They seemed unnaturally huge. Fargo realized it was only the man, and knew who it was.

Werner.

Big or not, a knife to the throat would kill him like it would any man. Fargo gripped the toothpick so tight his knuckles hurt and coiled to spring.

Every now and then Werner bent down, as if looking for tracks. He rode with his hand on his revolver. Up close, he was a mountain.

Werner would pass within a few yards to Fargo's left.

Fargo let him go by, pushed up, took two swift strides, and leaped. His aim was to hook his left arm over Werner's shoulder while simultaneously thrusting the toothpick into Werner's gullet. It should have worked. On a smaller man it would have. But Werner was so big that Fargo misjudged his leap. He managed to clamp a hand on Werner's shoulder but didn't jump high enough to stab him in the neck. So he stabbed him in the back, instead.

Werner tumbled. He didn't swear or cry out. He struck like a heavy boulder but was on his feet almost before Fargo. His big hand splayed to his holster and came away empty. His six-shooter had fallen loose.

Fargo attacked. He stabbed at Werner's chest, only to have his arm swatted aside. He figured Werner would shout for the others. Instead, Werner bunched those giant fists and waded in. Fargo ducked a blow that would have smashed his face in, pivoted, and drove the toothpick at Werner's ribs. He scored, too, but only a glancing strike. All Werner did was grunt.

Fargo tried to skip out of reach, but a sledgehammer caught him on the upper arm. Sent sprawling, he scrambled to his hands and knees. Too late, he glimpsed a foot arcing at his torso. He was booted so hard, it was a miracle his chest didn't stave in.

The stars and the earth changed places a few times, and he came to rest on his back.

A behemoth loomed above him.

"Puny scout," Werner said. "I don't care what the boss wants. I'm going to stomp you to bits."

Fargo saw a boot raised over his head. He threw himself aside and Werner came after him, slamming his boot down again and again. Suddenly reversing direction, Fargo rolled into Werner's other leg.

Werner tottered and flung out his arms to steady himself.

Pushing up, Fargo stabbed him in the thigh.

Werner growled like a bear and backpedaled. Pressing one hand to the wound, he raised his other hand to his face. "I'm tired of you cutting me."

Springing, Fargo sought to bury the blade again, into the big man's side. A backhand about fractured his cheek. Down he went, struggling to stay conscious. He felt his wrist gripped in a vise. Another hand locked on his throat and he was bodily lifted into the air.

"Got you," Werner gloated. He smiled and coughed, and dark rivulets flowed from both corners of his mouth. "What?" he said, and glanced down at himself. "What did you do to me?"

Fargo had switched the toothpick to his other hand and driven it between Werner's ribs.

"No one kills me. Not you. Not anybody."

Fargo couldn't breathe. He punched the arm that held him by the throat, but he might as well have punched an oak.

Werner did more coughing. He hunched forward so they were nose to nose, intense concentration on his face. "Die, little man."

Fargo struggled. He hit. He kicked. His consciousness swam, and he was on the cusp of being cast into oblivion when he became aware that his knees had struck the ground. Blinking, he realized Werner had fallen to his own knees.

"Die, damn you!"

The stars faded out and all Fargo saw was blackness. He clawed at the fingers on his neck, or thought he did. A strange sensation came over him, as if he were falling into a well. He fell and fell. The last thing he remembered thinking was "This is a damn sorry way to die."

# 28

With a start Fargo opened his eyes. Overhead, stars sparkled. He sucked in a breath, tried to sit up, and involuntarily groaned. He was awash in pain. He swallowed and grimaced. His throat was on fire. Turning his head, he gave another start.

Werner's face wasn't a hand's width from his. Werner's eyes were wide in shock, his mouth agape.

Scrambling back, Fargo sat up. He looked around. None of the others had shown up. He slid to Werner and probed. The big German was soaked in blood. Evidently the toothpick had severed an artery or a vein.

"I'll be damned," Fargo croaked. He got to his knees and commenced to pat the ground. The toothpick had to be there somewhere. He was at it awhile before his fingers brushed the hilt. Wiping the blade on his pants, he slid it into his ankle sheath.

Fargo stood. With a little luck he'd be back in Inferno in under an hour. He looked around for Werner's horse and only then realized it was gone. He'd have to walk.

"Figures," he muttered.

Tilting his head back, Fargo found the Big Dipper. The bottom two stars in the dipper always pointed to the North Star. Once he knew north, the other points of the compass were easy. He started walking south toward the road.

Somewhere a coyote wailed. Otherwise, the night was still. There wasn't even a mosquito to buzz about Fargo's head.

The desert seemed dead but the lifelessness was deceptive. Rattlesnakes hunted at night. Some lizards only came out after dark, too. The rats, as well, both the ones that could hop like rabbits and the ones that hoarded things. Night was also when foxes and bobcats were abroad.

Fargo was almost to the road when he stopped cold in his tracks. Ahead was . . . something. He couldn't quite make it out.

Warily advancing, he thought it must be a rider, but it turned out to be a horse by itself.

The horse stood with its head hung low in fatigue. It must have caught his scent, and looked back at him.

"Easy," Fargo said. He patted its neck and moved to the saddle. Unless he was mistaken, this was Werner's animal. The saddlebags caught his eye. He opened the first, thinking he might find jerky to eat or, better yet, a flask of red-eye. Instead, when he slid his hand in, his fingers met the cold steel of a revolver.

Fargo pulled it out. "I'll be damned." It was his Colt. He twirled it, forward and backward, then checked that there were pills in the wheel. How Werner ended up with it puzzled him until he recollected that it had been Werner who disarmed him at the cabin

It was too much to expect the Henry to be in the scabbard, and it wasn't. But Fargo saw the stock and barrel of a rifle were jutting from either end of Werner's bedroll. Sliding it out, Fargo smiled. "Here you are," he said.

Climbing on, Fargo reined toward town. His confidence had swelled tenfold. Let them try to stop him now and there would be hell to pay.

Fargo brought the horse to a trot. That time of night, he had the road to himself. The town, too—when he got there, the streets were empty.

Melissa's front door hung wide open.

Fargo closed and bolted it and went to her bedroom. She had rolled over onto her other side and was still snoring, oblivious to all that had happened.

The stove had gone out; the coffeepot was cold. Fargo settled for a glass of water.

He made himself comfortable on the settee, the Henry cradled in his arms. He was happy as could be to have the rifle and his Colt back. Touching his hair, he grumbled, "I wish I had my damn hat."

It must have been an hour later that he drifted off.

Sounds from the kitchen woke him. The grandfather clock in the corner told him it was past seven. Annoyed at himself for sleeping past daybreak, he sat up and stretched. He was sore practically everywhere. His ribs, where he had been kicked, hurt with every movement.

Aromas wafting down the hall tantalized him. Eggs, he would bet, with sausage instead of bacon. Plus a fresh batch of coffee.

Bundled in her robe, Melissa was bustling about like a bumblebee. "Good morning," she greeted him with a smile. "Sleep well?"

"Not as well as you."

"That's too bad. I rarely have trouble sleeping. I don't let things worry me to where I would."

Fargo leaned the Henry against the wall by the door. "Having everybody in town die from lack of salt isn't something to worry about?" He took a cup from her cupboard.

"Of course it is, silly."

"One thing I never am," Fargo said, "is that."

"I only mean we shouldn't fret ourselves to death." Melissa scooped eggs onto a plate. "Some folks, that's all they do. They worry from the moment they open their eyes in the morning until they close them at night. What's the point to that?"

"It gives them an excuse to bite their nails."

Melissa laughed. "Only you would think of a thing like that. But you have a point. My sister is a nervous Nellie and bites her nails to the quick."

Filling the cup, Fargo sipped. The coffee was steaming hot, just what he needed. It seared him to his toes. and just like that, a lot of the hurt faded and his brain began to work again. "I don't know what I'd do without this."

"Coffee?" Melissa said. "I've never met anyone who drinks as much as you. No wonder you can't sleep."

"That's what making love is for. To tire you out so you can."

Melissa ignored that and said, "Coffee isn't your only vice. You're powerful fond of whiskey, too, I've noticed. Which do you prefer more?"

Fargo hadn't given it any thought. "If I had to go without, I reckon I'd give up the Monongahela."

"That surprises me."

"It surprises me, too."

Melissa set the eggs on the table and went back for the sausage. "I'm excited about today."

"You're looking forward to taking a bullet?"

"Has anyone ever told you that you can be as sarcastic as hell?"

"Me?" Fargo said.

"Some people have to work at it, but with you it comes naturally," Melissa observed. She was going to say more but loud pounding on her front door caused her to stiffen. "My word! Who can that be?"

Fargo set down the china cup and scooped up the Henry and went with her. The pounding continued until she opened the door.

"Marshal Bubaker!" Melissa exclaimed. "What on earth has gotten into you? What's all the ruckus?"

The lawman stared past her at Fargo. "I figured you'd be here if you were anywhere." He wasn't alone. Behind him were two men Fargo had never set eyes on before.

"What's wrong?" Melissa asked.

"Out of our way, Miss Gebhart," one of the men said. "We're going to thrash that son of a bitch."

# 29

"Thrash?" Fargo said.

Marshal Bubaker thrust out an arm, blocking the man from entering. "Hold on, Parker. We'll give him a chance to explain himself."

"What is there to explain?" the other townsman said. "We saw him with our own eyes."

"Saw him what?" Melissa asked.

Parker jabbed a finger at Fargo. "Saw your lover here ride out of town with Ignatius Crillian and his bunch. You damn hussy. You've been harboring an enemy in our very midst. I have half a mind—"

Fargo took a step and rammed the Henry's stock into Parker's gut. Parker doubled over, bleating, and grabbed at the jamb for support.

"Here now," Marshal Bubaker said. "You had no call to do that."

Fargo reached out and grabbed the front of Parker's shirt. "The only thing you got right," he growled, "is that you have half a mind." He shoved, and Parker fell against the other man, who held him up.

Melissa was crimson with embarrassment. "How could you talk to me like that, Mr. Parker? I've had tea with your wife."

"Never again," Parker spat. "If she lets you in our home, I'll take a switch to her. Just see if I don't."

"You brought him here to insult me?" Melissa said to Bubaker.

The lawman winced as if she had struck him. "I brought him to get to the bottom of his claim that Fargo rode out of town with Crillian."

"I did," Fargo said.

Melissa and Marshal Bubaker and the man holding Parker up all said at the same time, "What?"

"He made me go with him at gunpoint. Seems he found out about the plan to take over the salt lick. He figured that without me, you'd change your minds."

"A likely story," Parker spat.

Bubuaker didn't look convinced, either. "Just a danged minute. If he wanted you out of the way, why didn't he just kill you?"

"He was keeping me alive for his boss."

"His what?" Melissa said.

"Everyone knows this is all Crillian's doing," Marshal Bubaker said. "He's not working for someone else."

"I thought so, too, based on your say-so," Fargo said. "You were wrong."

Parker snorted. "Can't you see he's making this up? He was caught and it's the only way to save his hide."

"I don't know what I see," Marshal Bubaker said.

"Believe me or not," Fargo said. "What matters more is that they know you're coming. They'll be waiting."

"Hell," Bubaker said.

"This must be part of their scheme," Parker said. "To talk us out of taking the lick from them. They're scared, is what it is."

"Of you?" Fargo said, and laughed.

"You're not helping things," Marshal Bubaker said.

"Let him insult me," Parker said. "I don't care. Once I spread the word, no one in town will want anything to do with him."

"We're not letting him lead us to the salt lick—that's for damn sure," the other townsman said. "We'd likely ride into a trap."

"That's telling him, Seymour," Parker said.

Marshal Bubaker shook his head. "I don't know. I trust Fargo. It sounds loco that they didn't kill him, I admit, but he went out there once for us and almost didn't make it back."

"We only have his word on that," Parker said.

"And we know what that's worth," Seymour threw in.

Fargo was close to losing his temper again. "Were you two born with your heads up your asses or have you had to work at it?"

Melissa chortled.

"Laugh all you want, missy," Parker said, straightening. "But when this is over, everyone will be taking a good, hard look at you. And they might not like what they see." He nudged Seymour. "Come on, it's plain our tin star isn't going to do anything."

Marshal Bubaker watched them walk off, saying, "This is bad. They'll cause all kinds of trouble."

"So long as none of it ends up on Melissa's doorstep," Fargo said.

Melissa blushed again and said softly, "Thank you, Skye."

The lawman coughed. "Enough romance. This is serious. If Crillian really knows we're coming—"

"He does," Fargo said.

"—we'll be slaughtered," Bubaker finished. He gazed down the street. "What do I do?" he asked, more to himself than to them. "How can I prevent a bloodbath?"

"Call the attack off."

"I don't know if I can. I don't know if they'll listen to me. Everyone is all worked up about taking the salt lick over. You know how much we need the salt."

"Talk to the mayor," Fargo said. "Make him see sense."

Marshal Bubaker nodded and worriedly left them.

"I can't get over how brazen Crillian was, coming into town after you," Melissa commented. "And to my very doorstep."

"He can ride in here anytime he wants," Fargo said. "What does he have to be afraid of?"

"That's not fair. You make us sound like sheep."

"You are."

"That's harsh."

Fargo was blunt with her. "Hell, hardly any of you can shoot. We'll be lucky if just one of us makes it back from the salt lick." He frowned. "That includes me."

# 30

Fargo didn't let it affect his appetite. He ate half a dozen eggs, four sausages, and two pieces of toast smeared with butter, and downed five cups of coffee.

Melissa picked at her food and hardly said a word.

They were wrapping the meal up when there was another knock on the front door. Melissa went to answer it and came back with Marshal Bubaker and Mayor Hoffstedder at her heels.

"I tried and I tried," the lawman said. "I talked until I was blue in the face, and it did no good."

"Don't be so hard on yourself," Hoffstedder said.

Bubaker looked at Fargo and motioned at the mayor. "Talk to him, will you? Maybe you can do a better job of it."

"The issue has been settled," Hoffstedder said. "We listened to everything our marshal had to say, and took a vote. The attack is still on."

Fargo had an inspiration. "Would it hurt to delay it a day or two? Crillian might think you've called it off and let down his guard."

"It's now or never, as the saying goes," Mayor Hoffstedder said. "We might lose our courage if we wait."

Fargo gave him credit for at least being honest about it.

"Is there anything we can do that will give us an edge now that we've lost the element of surprise?" Marshal Bubaker asked.

Fargo had been thinking about that as he ate. "Do you have any black powder? A keg or two we can use?"

"I wish," Bubaker said. "We barely have enough ammunition."

"How about kerosene?"

"That we have," the lawman said.

"Have everyone who can bring some."

"Kerosene?" Mayor Hoffstedder scoffed. "To what end? Are you going to try and set the cabin on fire?"

“No,” Fargo said. “Have them bring old towels and blankets and anything else that can burn.”

“I don’t see what good that will do,” Hoffstedder said.

“I think I do,” Marshal Bubaker said. He nodded. “I’ll spread the word. We’re still heading out about noon. That gives us plenty of time.” Once again, he hurried off.

The mayor, though, lingered. “I’ve heard about Crillian paying you a visit. And your claim that he’s not in this alone. That he works for someone else.”

“Skye wouldn’t lie,” Melissa said.

“Skye, is it?” Hoffstedder said. “But never mind about that. I don’t share your confidence in him.”

“What has he done that gives you cause not to?”

“Your friend here has shown a remarkable knack for survival,” Mayor Hoffstedder said. “Some might call it miraculous. And when something is too good to be true, it usually is.” He wheeled on a heel and departed.

Melissa got up and began to clear the dishes. “I’m sorry. Here you are helping us, and the people you’re trying to help don’t trust you.”

About to refill his coffee cup, Fargo shrugged.

Melissa carried what was left of the eggs and sausage to the counter and came back. “I wouldn’t hold it against you if you said to hell with it, and rode out.”

Fargo had considered that, for all of ten seconds. He refilled his cup with coffee one last time.

Melissa put his dirty plate on top of hers, piled their silverware, and took them to the counter, too. “Cat got your tongue?” She turned to come back and glanced toward the hallway. Stopping cold, she blurted, “It can’t be.”

Fargo turned in his chair.

*“Bonjour,”* Jaffer said. He was holding a revolver and was his usual dapper self. “Have you missed me?”

“You dare?” Melissa said. “In broad daylight?”

“Everyone is so busy, mademoiselle,” Jaffer said, “that no one noticed me.” He entered the kitchen but stayed well back from the table. “You don’t seem as surprised to see me as she does.”

“I knew you’d show up sooner or later,” Fargo said. “We have unfinished business.”

“Indeed we do. Set your pistol on the floor and slide it away from you.”

Scowling, Fargo did.

*"Bien,"* Jaffer said. "Now we can get to it."

"You're going to shoot us in my own house?" Melissa said.

"I have been instructed to put him down," Jaffer said. "You have the misfortune of being with him. Such is life, eh?"

Fargo placed his hand on his cup. "I have a question."

"You may ask it," Jaffer said. "Consider it the last request of the condemned."

"Do you work for the same person Ignatius Crillian does?"

"I see no harm in saying that no, I do not."

"Do you know who hired Crillian?" Fargo asked, sliding his cup a couple of inches.

"My employer has told me, yes. I confess to being considerably surprised."

"Hold on," Melissa said. "I'm confused. Who hired you? What reason did they have?"

"I'm afraid I can't say who. As to why, I am to see that their interests in this matter are carried out."

"What interests?"

"Again, I am afraid I can't say."

Fargo idly placed his hand at the bottom of the cup. "My guess is it's someone here in town."

Jaffer smiled and took a step nearer. "You have deduced that much, have you? The chickens are so fixed on Crillian, they never think there might be a second party involved."

"Chickens?" Melissa said.

"Have you never seen one with its head chopped off?" Jaffer said. "It will run around awhile, going nowhere."

"I'm still confused."

"I will solve that for you," Jaffer said. "In a very short while you won't have a care in the world." He took another step. "You'll be dead."

# 31

Sudden pounding on the front door took them all by surprise.

Melissa stiffened and put her hand to her throat.

Jaffer partly turned and inadvertently took his revolver off Fargo. "Who can that be?"

Fargo made his move. He was out of his chair and around the table in a bound. Jaffer spun, and Fargo hurled the hot coffee at Jaffer's face. It struck Jaffer in the eyes just as the pistol went off. Dropping the cup, Fargo slammed his fist against the smaller man's chin. Jaffer was knocked back but stayed on his feet. Fargo grabbed his wrist before Jaffer could fire again and, locked together, they struggled. Fargo was bigger and heavier. It should have been easy but it wasn't. Jaffer was a tiger. He fought with incredible strength. Grappling, locked together, they collided with the wall.

Melissa yelled but Fargo didn't catch what she said.

Jaffer hissed in fury and resorted to his legs. He kicked Fargo in the shin. He kicked Fargo in the thigh. He gave a slight hop and kicked at Fargo's gut.

Fargo shifted and Jaffer's foot caught him on the ribs. Fighting him was like fighting a jackrabbit. Fargo had never gone up against anyone who kicked so much. He rammed a knee at Jaffer's head but Jaffer avoided it.

Determined that this would be their last encounter, Fargo hooked a foot behind Jaffer's leg and tried to trip him. Somehow, Jaffer reversed the tactic, and the next moment Fargo was on a knee and the little man aimed a vicious kick at his throat.

Fargo took it on the chin. Twisting, he slammed Jaffer down and wrenched on Jaffer's arm. The revolver went skittering. Fargo let go of Jaffer's arm and drove his fist at Jaffer's jaw, but the man truly was a jackrabbit. Dodging, Jaffer sprang high into the air and kicked Fargo in the head.

Fargo fell back, clawing at his pant leg.

Whirling, Jaffer snatched at his six-gun. Out of nowhere Melissa was there and kicked it away. Seizing her, Jaffer shoved her at Fargo and dived for the revolver.

By then Fargo had the Arkansas toothpick in his hand. With his left arm he swept Melissa aside even as his right arm arced and the toothpick became a gleaming streak that imbedded itself in Jaffer's throat.

Jaffer's eyes grew wide in astonishment. Clutching at the toothpick, he reeled.

His legs melted from under him and he collapsed onto his side.

Using his boot, Fargo rolled him over.

Jaffer looked up. He tried to speak but all that came out was blood.

"Oh, you poor man," Melissa said. "I'm so sorry."

Fargo didn't see what she had to be sorry about. Squatting, he pulled the toothpick out and wiped the blade on Jaffer's suit.

Gurgling, Jaffer raised a bloody hand. Again he tried to speak.

"Who were you working for?" Fargo asked. Not that he expected an answer.

Jaffer's arm went slack and his eyes began to glaze.

"I've never seen anyone die before," Melissa said.

"You'll see a lot die if you go to the salt lick," Fargo predicted.

At the sudden sound of footsteps, he whirled, thinking that this time Jaffer had brought help. But no, it was Marshal Bubaker, who froze and gaped at the body. "It's that little fella you told me about."

"It was," Fargo said.

"I can't leave you alone for five minutes without something happening."

Melissa tore her gaze from Jaffer. "You came into my home without being invited?"

"I'm sorry," Bubaker said. "I knocked but no one answered. It's important. It's about him." He nodded at Fargo. "The mood out there is ugly. Parker and Seymour have been spouting off and working folks up. It's best if he doesn't show himself on the street for a while."

"He's willing to help us and this is how we treat him?" Melissa said.

"You can't hardly blame them," Marshal Bubaker said. "A lot of them are so sick, they're not thinking straight. They want Crillian and anyone they think is working with him gone more than anything."

"But Skye is on our side," Melissa persisted.

"You know that and I know that, but they don't know him as well as we do." Bubaker stepped to Jaffer. "I'll get some men to haul the body to the undertaker's. Crillian will be mad as hell when he hears we've killed one of his gun hands."

"He said he wasn't," Melissa said.

"Wasn't what?"

"Working for Crillian. He claimed he was working for someone else."

The lawman scratched his chin. "Either he was lying, or this mess is more complicated than I reckoned. If not Crillian, then who? And why?"

"Crillian claimed he's working for someone, too," Fargo reminded him.

"For the same person? Or were they working for somebody different?" Bubaker swore, then caught himself. "I can't make hide nor hair of this. And I'm not going to try. If I think any harder, my head will explode." He touched his hat brim to Melissa. "Ma'am," he said, and clomped out.

"What do you make of it all?" Melissa asked.

"I don't yet," Fargo said. He didn't have enough pieces of the puzzle. Someone had hired Crillian to force the town to pay an outrageous price for salt they couldn't do without. It seemed to him that Jaffer's whole purpose had been to keep him from helping the townsfolk. Or maybe it was to stop anyone from helping them.

"I hope we make sense of it soon," Melissa remarked. "To prevent more bloodshed." She tugged on the belt of her robe. "Now if you'll excuse me, I don't want anyone else to see me like this. I'm going to wash up and get dressed."

Fargo poured more coffee and sat at the table. He went over everything that had happened since he got there. There must be a clue somewhere to who was behind it all.

He was still pondering when three men came in to cart Jaffer off. They gave him suspicious looks but held their peace.

When Melissa returned, she wore a riding outfit and a flat-brimmed hat. "You've been sitting there this whole time? What have you been doing?"

"Trying to figure it all out."

"Have you?"

Fargo shook his head.

"Too bad. We're running out of time."

"Tell me something I don't know," Fargo said.

# 32

Storekeepers, clerks, bartenders, the butcher, the barber, the undertaker, the mayor, the banker, and more, all with revolvers strapped around their waists and brandishing rifles, sat their mounts in the street in front of the marshal's office awaiting word to head out. Some of the women wore outfits similar to Melissa Gebhart's. Others wore dresses. They, too, were armed, many holding their rifles in awkward imitation of the way many of the men held theirs.

In the shade of the overhang, Marshal Bubaker turned to Fargo and asked, "What do you think?"

"Pitiful comes to mind," Fargo said.

"There are enough of us that if we can sneak in close, we stand a prayer."

"Maybe you won't have to."

"How's that again?"

"Maybe Crillian and his gun hands will see you coming and laugh themselves to death."

Parkinson brought his mount up close. He wore expensive hunting clothes, the kind an Easterner might wear. A rifle in a special case hung from his saddle. "What's the holdup, Marshal?" he asked. "We've been ready to ride for ten minutes now."

"The last straggler just got here," Bubaker said.

Mayor Hoffstedder joined them. His backside flopped and his legs flapped with every step his horse took. "Are we ready?"

"That's what I wanted to know," Parkinson said.

"A quick announcement and we'll be on our way," Bubaker said. He moved past them and faced the townsfolk. Waving his arms to get their attention, he hollered, "Everyone quiet down."

The murmur of hushed voices faded.

"We've been all through this but it doesn't hurt to bring it up again," Bubaker said. "This is a dangerous undertaking. Do exactly as you're told at all times. Anything you're confused about, come see me."

"Or me," Mayor Hoffstedder said.

Parker and Seymour, the pair who had given Fargo a hard time earlier, were across the street with several other men. Parker pointed at Fargo and yelled, "Some of us don't want him leading us. We don't trust him."

"Then stay here," Marshal Bubaker said.

"I trust him," Melissa told the others. "He won't let any harm come to us if he can help it."

Fargo wished she hadn't said that. He'd do what he could but, as he'd pointed out several times, they were fleas attacking bears. It worried him, how sickly some of them looked. Several could barely sit their saddles. "It's not too late to change your minds," he said quietly to Bubaker.

"No," the lawman said. "We have to do it." He turned to Parker and the other malcontents. "What will it be? Join us or stay, but make up your minds."

"We'll go," Parker said begrudgingly.

"But we don't like it," Seymour said.

With Fargo out in front, the Inferno "army" got under way. The heat, as usual, was withering. Fargo hadn't gone a quarter of a mile when he was slick with sweat. Every time he glanced back, people were sucking on their canteens. It prompted him to say to Bubaker, "If they're not careful, they'll run out of water before we get there."

The lawman looked over his shoulder, frowned, and nodded. "I'll talk to them." Reining around, he went from rider to rider.

Fargo missed his hat more than ever. He would look for it once this whole mess was over.

A horse came alongside the Ovaro.

"Have any of them given you any trouble?" Fargo asked.

"Not a word," Melissa said. "They're too preoccupied. None of them has ever been in a fight before. This will be their first."

"And maybe their last."

"I'm more worried about the condition some of them are in. Mrs. Franklyn is so sick, she almost passed out. And there are a couple of men who can barely hold their rifles."

"They should have stayed in Inferno."

Melissa ran a hand across her brow. "Their homes, their families, their very lives are at stake. They want to do their part."

"They can't do anyone any good dead."

"Must you always be so harsh? Personally, I think it's noble of them to put their lives in danger."

"All of you have."

"Not by choice. It's do or die and we want our town to live." Melissa looked over at him. "You're the only one of us who has no vested stake in the outcome. You could go your own way and no one would hold it against you."

"I would."

"You're awful hard on yourself."

"It's not that," Fargo said, and elaborated. "I have what you might call rules I live by. If someone hits me, I hit back. If someone tries to blow out my wick, I put windows in their skull."

"Most folks call that getting revenge," Melissa said with a slight grin.

"I call it standing up for myself."

"Manly pride," Melissa said, and laughed as if it were funny.

"A man who won't be trod on is being true to his nature. Turning the other cheek is for weak sisters."

"A lot of us aren't as strong as you," Melissa said. "We're timid and can't help it."

"One thing I've never been," Fargo said, "is that."

"My grandmother used to say that cowards are born that way."

"Turning tail is a choice. Our legs don't run unless we tell them to."

"You have a point. But it's hard for everyone not to give in to fear."

"Give in to it at the salt lick and we're all goners," Fargo said.

# 33

The ride was hell.

Fargo had to constantly slow so that those who fell behind could catch up. Several times he drew rein to wait while someone retched.

At their snail's pace it would be well past dark when they got to the salt lick. Which worked in their favor. But he had to wonder how many of them would be able to fight worth a damn.

Now and then Marshal Bubaker took it on himself to call a halt so everyone could rest. Along about the third time, Fargo dismounted to stretch his legs, then squatted to wait. When a shadow fell across him, he looked up and frowned. "What the hell do you want?"

Parker and Seymour were with two others. All four had the look of men on the peck.

"We aim to give you a piece of our mind," Parker said.

"Go pester somebody else," Fargo said.

"You don't tell us what to do," Seymour said. "We're not the marshal. We don't bow and scrape to the great scout."

Fargo wasn't in the mood for their nonsense. He tried counting to ten in his head and got to two.

Parker put his hands on his hips. "We'll be watching you, mister. Anything suspicious, we'll put lead into you quicker than you can blink."

"Big brag for a bunch of turtles," Fargo said.

Seymour's beady eyes narrowed in resentment. "Keep insulting us and see what happens."

"How about I do this instead?" Fargo said, and sweeping erect, he rammed his fist into Seymour's gut, doubling him over. Shoving him aside, Fargo sprang at Parker. Caught flatfooted, Parker tried to raise his arms to defend himself. Fargo slugged him.

The other two were rooted in disbelief.

Shouts broke out.

Fargo didn't take his eyes off Parker, who suddenly lunged, his fists flying. Fargo blocked the blows and let fly with a right cross and a left uppercut. Parker teetered. A straight-arm to the chin dropped him.

Fargo whirled to confront the others. "Anyone else?"

Seymour, on one knee, was gasping and waving a hand. "No more," he said.

"How about you two?" Fargo growled at the other two.

"Not me, mister," one said.

The other shook his head.

Marshal Bubaker ran up, huffing from the heat. "What the hell is going on? I told all of you to leave Fargo be."

"We just wanted to talk," Seymour said sullenly.

"And he attacked us," Parker said, rubbing his jaw.

"On your horses," the lawman commanded. "We're moving out."

The incident didn't improve Fargo's mood any. It didn't help that the enormity of what he was doing had him on edge. Granted, attacking the salt lick was their idea. But by midnight a lot of them would be worm food.

They left the road to circle into the hills. Some of the horses were as worn as the riders, and plodded along with their heads hung low. The heat was only part of it. A lot of these mounts had seldom been ridden long distances, and were coddled with stalls and by being grain-fed.

In that regard horses were like people. A soft life made for a soft horse. It was well known that wild horses were hardier than their pampered cousins. Likewise, the Ovaro. The stallion had been tempered in the forge of Fargo's never-ending wanderings.

He was glad when the hills appeared. As the last vestige of sun fled the sky, he guided them in and called a halt.

Everyone was nervous and anxious. When they spoke, it was in hushed tones.

Marshal Bubaker, Mayor Hoffstedder, and the banker materialized, and the lawman asked, "Do we wait for it to get darker?"

"That," Fargo said, "and I want to scout ahead on foot."

"Who do you want to go with you?" the mayor asked.

"Me, myself, and I."

"What if something happens to you? Besides, some of the others won't like it if you go alone. They might think you're going to warn Crillian that we're here."

"Odds are he already knows," Fargo said.

"Don't talk like that," Parkinson said. "You'll jinx us."

"Who goes with you?" Hoffstedder pressed the issue.

"I'll take the marshal," Fargo said.

Bubaker didn't appear happy. "Is that wise? One of us should keep an eye on Parker and Seymour and their friends or they might stir up trouble."

"Fine," Fargo said in annoyance. He pointed at the banker. "I'll take you."

"Me?" Parkinson blurted. "Why on earth would you want to? I'm no good with a gun. I'd be useless."

"Take me instead," Hoffstedder volunteered.

"You?" Fargo said in surprise. In his estimation the mayor was just as worthless as the banker.

"Why not? I'm willing. And the marshal doesn't need me to help keep Parker and Seymour in line."

Fargo hesitated. He would rather go alone. But if that would cause problems for Bubaker, he might as well let the mayor come.

The mayor hefted his rifle. "Just so you know. I've never shot anyone but I'm more than willing to do so. In fact, if I wasn't in politics, I'd probably be a soldier. I always saw myself as a general leading a charge on a battlefield."

"You?" Marshal Bubaker said before Fargo could.

"Why not?" Hoffstedder said. "When I was little I liked to read about the Romans and their wars. This might sound sacrilegious, but I've often wondered if I might have been a Roman general in a previous life. I sometimes have vivid dreams of leading a legion of Roman soldiers against Hannibal and his elephants. In one of my dreams I captured an elephant and rode it."

"You?" Marshal Bubaker said again.

Hoffstedder turned to Fargo. "Am I acceptable to you or not?"

"You can come," Fargo said. "But leave your elephant here."

Bubaker laughed.

The gray of twilight was spreading. Overhead, the first few stars sparkled like fireflies.

Fargo shucked the Henry from his saddle scabbard and worked the lever to feed a cartridge into the chamber. "Stay behind me," he said to Hoffstedder. "Stop when I stop. Go to ground when I go to ground. Don't talk unless I say you can. Savvy?"

"I'll be your second shadow."

A lot of apprehensive looks, and a few unfriendly ones, were thrown Fargo's way as he led the mayor off.

"Isn't this exciting?" Hoffstedder whispered.

Fargo stopped and Hoffstedder bumped into him. Turning, Fargo poked him in the chest. "What about 'don't talk' didn't you understand?"

"Sorry. I'm just all tingly with excitement."

"Maybe you should go back."

"Bear with me. Please. I've never done anything like this before. You're used to it. You fight redskins and the like. The only one I've ever fought with is my wife. And she usually wins. She can be quite fearsome."

Fargo muttered an oath under his breath.

"What was that?"

"Not another peep."

Hoffstedder ran a finger across his mouth. "My lips are sealed from here on out."

"Bet me," Fargo grumbled, and cat-footed on.

Above them the gray became black. They reached the last hill without being shot at or challenged, and Fargo flattened to crawl to where he'd be able to see the cabin and the lean-to.

"Must we?" Hoffstedder said.

"Get down, damn you."

"I don't think I will," Hoffstedder said, and to Fargo's amazement, he pointed his rifle at him and thumbed back the hammer.

# 34

"What in hell do you think you're doing?"

*"Shhhh,"* Hoffstedder said, and laughed. "You wouldn't want them to hear you." He took a step back, holding his rifle steady. "Do yourself a favor. Set your Henry on the ground, put your pistol next to it, and stand up with your hands in the air and I won't shoot you."

Fargo's gut balled into a knot. "Damn me if you're not serious."

"Never more so," Hoffstedder said. "You might think I won't

shoot after what I told you a bit ago. But for three thousand dollars, I'll gladly squeeze this trigger. Hell, for that much, I'd shoot my fearsome wife."

It had been Fargo's experience that a greenhorn with a gun was ten times as dangerous as an experienced shooter. "You mind explaining what this is about?" Fargo said as he raised his hand from the Henry.

"It's what it's always been about," Hoffstedder said. "I'm also mad at you for killing my ace in the hole."

"Your what?"

"Jaffer. He was in my employ. Insurance, you might say, against being betrayed. Now I must rely on my own wits and ability, such as they are."

Fargo was so tired of having guns pointed at him, he almost went for his Colt. But even if he got off his shot, Hoffstedder still might fire, and at that range even an imbecile couldn't miss. He set his Colt next to the Henry.

"Excellent. On your feet and march to the cabin."

"They'll shoot me on sight."

"Not if I give a yell. Start moving."

Fargo saw that not one but two fires had been kindled near the lean-to. Only a couple of men sat at each. The cabin window was brightly lit, and shadows moved across it.

"You must be wondering where the rest are," Hoffstedder said.

An awful premonition filled Fargo.

Raising his voice, Hoffstedder called out, "Crillian! Where are you? It's me. Hoffstedder. I've brought a guest."

The men at the lean-to sprang to their feet. Simultaneously, the darkness all around disgorged furtive figures, Dreel and Ramirez and Willy among them.

"I don't believe it," Dreel said to Hoffstedder. "A no-account weakling like you got the better of him?"

"It was child's play," Hoffstedder boasted. "I completely pulled the wool over his eyes."

"You must feel dumb as a rock right about now," Dreel said to Fargo.

"You have no idea."

The gun hands parted and through them strode Ignatius Crillian. "Well, look who it is," he said with a smile. "The gent we can't wait to shoot to pieces."

"Let me go first," Willy said, eagerly raising his six-gun.

"You do and I'll shoot you," Crillian said. "The boss wants to talk to him, remember?"

"Hoffstedder isn't behind all this?" Fargo had leaped to that conclusion, although for the life of him he couldn't imagine what Hoffstedder was up to.

"Him?" Dreel said, and uttered a cold bark of a laugh. "He can't lead his own ass to the outhouse."

"Must you?" Hoffstedder said.

"Enough," Crillian snapped at Dreel. "The mayor is an ally, and he's been of some use."

"I've been of great help," Hoffstedder said. "I warned you the good people of Inferno were attacking tonight, didn't I? So you can spring your little ambush."

"We're ready," Crillian said.

"I'll go back and tell them that Fargo is still scouting around and they're to stay put. That will give you plenty of time to surround them."

"It'll be like shootin' ducks in a barrel," Willy said.

"In a barrel or on the wing is all the same to me," Dreel said.

About to go, Hoffstedder turned to Ignatius Crillian. "You're taking Fargo to . . . him?"

"I don't know where he is. We'll hold Fargo until he gets here. For some reason he wants to talk to him."

"That loco bastard makes my skin crawl," Dreel remarked. "But he's payin' us and that's what counts."

"I do not trust him, amigo," Ramirez said.

Dreel smirked. "Hell, you don't trust anybody."

"Let's get the scout in the cabin." Crillian put an end to their small talk.

Seven gun hands hemmed Fargo. Dreel shoved him and said, "Get a move on."

Simmering, Fargo did.

"Nothin' to say?" Dreel taunted.

"He never does say much," Willy said. "He's one of those quiet ones you have to watch out for."

"It's the one who hired us we must watch out for," Ramirez said.

"There you go again," Dreel said.

"You don't believe me, amigo?"

"We've been pards how many years now and you ask me a thing like that?"

"This gent who hired you," Fargo said. "I don't suppose you'd tell me who he is?"

"Not a chance in hell. You're lucky he's curious about you. Were it up to me, I'd splatter your brains." Dreel glowered. "Which reminds me. Werner was another pard of mine, and you did him in."

"We found his body, señor," Ramirez said. "It made us very mad." He suddenly stopped and snapped his fingers. "Where is my head? How can I have forgot?"

"Forgot what?" Dreel asked.

"Search him. He must have a knife on him. Our friend Werner was stabbed and he did not carry a knife."

Willy and another man patted Fargo from collar to boots. It was the other one who found the ankle sheath and held the Arkansas toothpick up for all of them to see.

"Lookee here."

"You were right, Ramirez," Dreel said.

Fargo was shoved again and nearly tripped. When they reached the cabin, Dreel opened the door and a pair of gun hands roughly hauled Fargo inside. Boiling with fury, he did nothing that would earn him a bullet to the brainpan.

"You two stand guard outside," Ramirez said, pointing at those he'd picked. "If the scout so much as opens the door, shoot him."

"Who made you boss, Mex?" one of the men said. "We don't take orders from you."

Dreel took a step, his hands on his Remingtons. "You do now."

As they filed out, Ramirez turned. "I would not touch anything, were I you, amigo. The *demente zorro* who hired us would not like it." He closed the door after him.

"Insane fox?" Fargo said to himself. Leaning against the table, he took stock. He was weaponless, a prisoner, cut off from the rest, with no way to warn them. And unless he did, they would all soon die.

Fargo thought of Melissa and Bubaker. He moved to the window and peered out.

One of the guards appeared and motioned with his rifle.

Fargo stepped back, racking his brain. He could set the cabin on fire to try to draw them in and jump them. But if they were smart enough not to fall for his ruse, the fire and smoke might do him in.

The only other thing he could think of was to do what he did; he picked up a chair.

# 35

Fargo heaved it at the window. The glass shattered with a loud crash and before the pieces hit the floor, Fargo was in motion. He darted to the front door, flung it wide, and plunged out into the night. Out of the corner of his eye he saw that the two guards had rushed to the window. Too late, they realized the trick he'd played, and spun.

Fargo was around the corner before they could shoot. He figured the rest were on their way to deal with the townsfolk and were ahead of him somewhere.

The guards came after him. One hollered for him to stop but neither fired.

That puzzled him until it hit him that they couldn't. Any shooting and Bubaker and the others would hear and know that something had gone wrong.

Fargo pumped his legs, making for where he'd left the Henry and the Colt. There was a chance Hoffstedder hadn't gone back for them.

The guards weren't fast runners. Fargo quickly increased his lead and heard one of them call out to the other.

"Where did he get to?"

"I don't know."

Fargo didn't slow. Too many lives were at stake. He reached the spot where the Henry and Colt should be but they weren't there. Casting frantically about, he felt a wave of relief when metal glinted in the starlight. The Henry's brass receiver was like a mirror. Scooping it up, he groped and found the Colt.

Fargo ran on. He hoped to catch up to Crillian and company before they attacked the townspeople, but there was no sign of them.

He felt another wave of relief when he burst in among the people from Inferno. Most were seated on the ground, apparently waiting for him to return. Several cried out in alarm and raised their rifles.

"It's me," Fargo called out, although not too loudly. He saw Bubaker and raced over. "You're about to be attacked."

"What? The mayor was just here and said everything was fine and we're to wait to hear from you."

"He was lying. He's working with them." Fargo looked around. "Where did he get to?"

"I'm not sure," Marshal Bubaker said.

"Crillian and his gun hands will be here any minute."

"The hell you say."

"Have everyone lie flat and tell them not to move," Fargo said. "Have about ten face north, ten face south, you get the idea. The first person to spot the pack of killers spreads the word, but quietly."

Bubaker nodded and rushed to get it done.

Melissa appeared, and clasped Fargo's arm. "I'm glad you're back. I was so worried."

"Get down," Fargo said, and pulled her to the ground. In a few words he told her about the impending attempt to wipe them out.

"And you say the mayor is in it with them? What does he hope to gain?"

"Who the hell knows?"

She went to say something but Fargo put a hand to her mouth. He thought he'd heard something off in the dark. When the sound wasn't repeated, he moved his hand. "I thought it might be them."

"I can't believe it about the mayor," Melissa whispered. "But now some of the things he's said make sense."

"What things?"

"Not that long ago some of us were talking about the next election, and how he was a shoo-in to win. And he looked up and down the street and said it was a shame."

"And?" Fargo said, straining his ears.

"Someone asked him why he said that, and Hoffstedder answered that sometimes circumstances dictate what we do, whether we want them to or not. I wondered what he was getting at."

Bubaker was talking to a last knot of townspeople.

"Another time," Melissa said, "at a town meeting a week or so before the trouble started, Hoffstedder mentioned that if it was up to him, everyone would move elsewhere and Inferno would become a ghost town. Someone said that was a fine thing for him to say, him being the mayor and all. Hoffstedder laughed and answered that we'd be lucky if the town lasted another year."

"He knew about Crillian."

"It would seem so. But why didn't he warn us? If we'd acted right away, we might have prevented all this."

"You can ask him yourself later on," Fargo said. Provided she, and Hoffstedder, were still alive.

A deathly quiet had fallen. Every last man and woman was flat on their stomachs. Rifles were pressed to shoulders.

"How much longer, do you think?" Melissa whispered.

"Your guess is as good as mine."

Many of the horses had their heads up and were staring to the east. Fargo looked but didn't see anything.

"I'm scared," Melissa whispered. "So are most of the people here, I'd warrant. We've never done anything like this."

"Stand up and jump up and down and yell a few times, why don't you?"

"Is that your way of telling me to be quiet?"

"It's better than slugging you."

The horses were still staring to the east. Fargo was about to crawl in that direction when someone came snaking toward him, moving clumsily and noisily.

"I want to hear about Hoffstedder," Parkinson said. "The marshal tells me he's switched sides."

"He's been with them from the start," Fargo guessed. He started to crawl off but Parkinson gripped his wrist.

"Hold on. I need to know everything. What did he say? Where did you see him last?"

"Not now."

Parkinson didn't let go. "Parker and Seymour think you murdered him."

"Why in hell would I do that?"

"They say you're lying. That you're the one working with Crillian."

"We've been all through that, you blockhead," Fargo said. "Any minute now—" He stopped.

A horse had whinnied.

To the east, a line of darkling shapes reared up and rushed to the attack.

# 36

"Here they come!" a townsman shouted.

All hell broke loose.

Gunfire blasted, a volley from the attackers. Most of their shots were high, and missed.

"Open fire! Open fire!" Marshal Bubaker bawled. He was the first of the defenders to do so, working his rifle like a madman.

Galvanized into action, those lying on the east side cut loose. Those lying to the north, west and south had to turn to shoot and were slower in adding to the thunder and to the flare of muzzle flashes.

Fargo aimed at an onrushing silhouette and fired. Jacking the Henry's lever, he aimed at another.

By now the gun hands had realized the townspeople were lying on the ground and were shooting lower. Men screamed and shrieked and cursed. The wail of a stricken woman pierced the din.

A voice bellowed commands. *Crillian,* Fargo thought. The attackers went to ground, too, but not before another was hit, pinwheeled as if drunk, and collapsed.

Beside Fargo, Melissa methodically worked her rifle.

Parkinson suddenly reared onto his knees, his hands to his chest. "I'm hit!" he cried, and was hit again, in the head. The impact pancaked him on his back.

Not far off another townsman thrashed in his death throes.

It was a shooting gallery for Crillian's crew. They were picking off the townsfolk with a clever tactic; several would fire at the same time at a defender's muzzle flash.

Fargo saw a figure heave up and fired. There was a screech and the gun-for-hire dropped.

So far Crillian hadn't thought to run their horses off. The next moment, though, they bolted on their own.

Another screech rent the night. Another townsman had died.

Fargo scrambled toward those to the east, intending to help them. He didn't realize Melissa was crawling with him until she bumped him. "Stay put," he hollered, and hurried on.

She came with him.

Fargo couldn't waste breath arguing. He fired at a flash and rolled in case an attacker fired back. One did, the lead thudding into the dirt inches from his head. He reached the ten townsfolk—nine men and a woman—who had been facing east and had borne the brunt of the violence. The first man he came on was dead. So was the second. Glancing about, he saw others who weren't moving. Only three or four were still alive. He turned to the woman, who was desperately trying to insert a cartridge, and put his mouth to her ear. "Get the hell out of here." He motioned at the middle of the square.

The woman looked at him, her eyes wide with fear she was struggling to contain. She smiled and nodded, and a slug struck her in the temple, cored her head, and burst out the other side.

Fargo snapped a shot at the shooter.

At his elbow, Melissa fired, too.

"Back away," Fargo said to her, and hollered it at the two men still firing. They were quick to retreat to join the rest.

The townsfolk to the north, west and south were putting up a spirited fight, but the gun hands were becoming bolder. One heaved onto his knees and cut loose with a revolver in each hand, firing so swiftly, the shots blended one into another. Dreel, Fargo reckoned, in a remarkable display of ambidextrous ability. He centered the Henry but the two-gun killer threw himself flat again.

Fargo backed away, shooting as he went. He glanced at Melissa and saw her moving as fast as she could while pressed as low as she could to keep from taking lead. Slowing to cover her, he worked the lever and squeezed the trigger. Nothing happened, the Henry was empty.

Rather than reload, Fargo resorted to his Colt. Curling the hammer as he drew, he snapped a shot at a charging shape. The man yipped like a kicked cur and toppled.

Rising into a crouch, Fargo backpedaled. He shot at a second figure, and a third.

By then he had reached the others.

The surviving townsfolk to the north, west and south were pouring fire at the hired guns.

With lightning clarity Fargo noticed two things. First, Crillian and his men were spreading out, no doubt to encircle the defenders. And second, barely half the townspeople were left. They were being picked to ribbons.

An instant decision was called for. Stay and fight and be decimated. Or flee and live to fight later.

Fargo saw Marshal Bubaker and skittered to him. Shouting to be heard, Fargo said, "If we stay we'll be wiped out. Get them out of here."

The lawman must have already realized the same thing. "Retreat!" he roared.

"Into the hills! Move! Move!"

Inferno's army needed little urging. Most fled in shameless terror. A handful, like Fargo, fired as they went to protect their backs.

Oddly, Ignatius Crillian didn't press his advantage. The shooting from his side stopped.

With only one cartridge left in the Colt, Fargo made it around a hill.

Melissa materialized at his side. "God, I was scared."

"Save your breath for running."

Fargo hadn't intended for the townspeople to go far but from the look of things they intended to keep going until they reached California. He yelled for them to stop.

"You can't blame them," Melissa huffed.

Someone else commenced hollering. It was Bubaker, screeching himself hoarse.

The survivors slowed from a run to a walk, and finally came to a halt.

Some were doubled over, panting. More than a few were wounded. He saw that Parker had been shot in the shoulder. There was no sign of Seymour.

Fargo set to reloading.

A few yards away, Marshal Bubaker had his hands on his knees and was cursing mightily. He stopped to declare, "How any of us made it out of there, I'll never know."

Fargo counted seventeen of the original thirty-nine still on their feet.

"That's all?" Melissa said when he told her. "How will we last through another attack?"

"We won't," the lawman panted.

"Talk a little louder, why don't you?" Fargo said. "So everyone can hear."

"Sorry," Bubaker said sheepishly. "I wasn't thinking."

The others were gathering around them, and the town baker said, "Don't apologize, Marshal. We should have listened to you and the scout. We bit off more than we could chew."

"I lost my husband," a woman said, and broke into tears. "I don't want to die, too. What will our children do?"

"Quiet down," Marshal Bubaker warned. "Do you want them to hear you?"

"They must know where we are," a man said.

From out of the night came a bellow, courtesy of Ignatius Crillian. "Do you hear me over there?"

"We're in for it now," the same man said.

# 37

The marshal went to answer but Fargo said, "No. Let me." He faced in the direction they had come. "We hear you, Crillian."

"Is that you, Fargo?"

"No, it's Melissa Gebhart."

No one laughed.

"Well, *Melissa*," Crillian called, "you have stepped in it. We have nine rifles trained on you."

"That's all the gun sharks you have left?" Fargo shouted.

"It's more than enough. We can wait until daybreak and pick you off or you can lay down your guns and surrender."

"We'll have to think about it."

"Don't think too long," Crillian said. "And don't try to sneak off. I've sent Willy and a couple of others around to the other side."

That made twelve, Fargo tallied them up. Crillian was right. More than enough to finish the townspeople off.

"We're trapped," a man wailed.

"God help us," said the woman who had lost her husband.

"What do we do?" another person asked, and all eyes swung to Marshal Bubaker.

The lawman, in turn, faced Fargo. "I'm open to ideas. We don't come up with one, we've lost the battle before we even reach the salt lick."

"Don't worry," Melissa said. "Skye will think of something."

Fargo could have kicked her. He was plumb out of brainstorms. "I'm as stumped as you. If we still had our horses, we could use the kerosene and towels we brought to make a lot of smoke and slip away."

"There has to be something," Marshal Bubaker said.

"We toss down our rifles but hold on to our revolvers. When they move in, we shoot them."

"*That's* your idea?" a man scoffed.

"It'll get us killed," said an older gent.

Parker picked that moment to shove through the others, his hand to his bloody shoulder. "I warned you back in town. I told you he was up to no good."

"Not that again," Marshal Bubaker said. "He could have been killed like any of us."

"Maybe, and maybe not," Parker said. "Maybe they tried not to hit him. Ever think of that?"

"That's preposterous," Melissa said.

"Is it?" someone asked.

"Here we go again," Bubaker said in disgust.

For some reason Willy popped into Fargo's head, and he repeated what Crillian had said. "Willy and a couple of others."

"What was that?"

"There are only three gun hands between us and the lick," Fargo said.

"So?" a woman replied.

"So we if make it to the cabin we can fort up," Fargo said. "It would give us a breather to think and plan."

Marshal Bubaker said, "I like the idea."

"I don't," Parker said. "It's another trick."

"Stay here, then, you stupid son of a bitch," Fargo said, and pushing him aside, he started toward the lick.

Some of the others—Melissa and the lawman among them—were quick to follow. Some hesitated, then came. Parker and another man stayed where they were, glaring.

Fargo moved cautiously, probing the darkness with his senses. Willy wasn't the brightest candle around; he was bound to give himself away.

Marshal Bubaker came up on his right. "I hope this works," he said. "We're goners if it doesn't."

Melissa, only a few steps behind them, said, "Trust in Skye. He knows what he's doing."

Fargo wished she would stop saying that.

The next two hills were close together, ideal for an ambush.

Fargo scanned the slopes. They were as barren of vegetation as most everywhere else. When the old man, Jensen, built that cabin, he must have hauled the trees from a long way off.

Movement brought Fargo to a stop. He couldn't be sure if it was a man or an animal. Since wildlife was so scarce, odds were it was Willy and his friends. He turned and whispered, "On that hill yonder. Pass it along."

The word spread down the line.

Fargo raised the Henry. He centered the barrel on whoever or whatever it was, and held his breath.

"Do it," Marshal Bubaker said.

Fargo fired. The blast was greeted by a yelp and the figure on the hill fell and rolled and then was up and moving toward some boulders. Fargo fired again and was sure he had missed.

On the other hill two rifles boomed.

"We rush them," Fargo said, and charged, firing furiously. He had a hunch Willy wouldn't stand his ground. Willy didn't impress him as having a lot of backbone.

Bubaker and Melissa were to either side, shooting. Behind them were others.

The firing from the second hill stopped. Fargo glimpsed figures skedaddling.

"Damn yellow curs," Marshal Bubaker spat.

Hurrying on, they reached the salt lick. It was more like a salt quarry, with a pit where salt had been scooped from the earth. On the far side stood the cabin, the broken window aglow.

"Do you see anyone?" Melissa asked.

Fargo didn't. Which didn't mean a thing. "More of them can be anywhere. Spread the word not to bunch up."

They worked their way around the pit. Fargo kept expecting gunfire to shatter the night but they drew near the cabin without another fight. A shadow moved across the window.

"Someone is in there," Marshal Bubaker said.

"Stay here." Fargo advanced alone. The lean-to was empty and the campfires had practically burned themselves out. The only sign of life was that shadow. He covered the last twenty feet at a run and pressed his back to the wall next to the door. He put his ear to it but heard nothing. About to reach for the latch, he froze when it moved without him touching it.

Someone was opening the door from the other side.

## 38

Fargo's curled his finger around he trigger. He figured it would be a gun hand or maybe Hoffstedder. Instead, an old man with long gray hair and a beard that fell to his waist scowled at the Henry and then at him. The oldster wore clothes that hadn't been washed in a month of Sundays. He had a bulbous nose with a wart on the tip and thick lips that curled in perpetual scorn.

"What do you want?" the old man demanded.

"Who are you?"

The man gestured at the Henry. "You fixin' to shoot me? If not, lower that damn thing."

"Are you one of Crillian's men?"

"That jackass?" The old man snorted. "I'm Jasper Jensen, sonny. This is my cabin, and you're on my land. Now are you goin' to lower that thing, or do I have to take it from you and beat you with it?"

"That would take some doing," Fargo said.

"Listen to you," Jensen said. "Kind of stoked on yourself, aren't you? Do you preen in the mirror a lot?"

"What?" Fargo said.

"Are you hard of hearin', too? I asked if you were in love with yourself. Wouldn't surprise me if you were. There's a lot of that goin' around these days, on account of all the stupid folks."

"What?"

"Why do you keep sayin' that? You must be simpleminded. That's common, too. People don't use their thinkers as much as they used to."

"How can you be alive?" Fargo asked in bewilderment.

Jensen looked down at his chest and took a couple of deep breaths. "See that? They call it breathin'. If you can do that, you're not dead."

Fargo lowered the Henry. "They told me you had been killed. That Ignatius Crillian did you in and took over the salt lick."

"Who told you that? Those knuckleheads in Inferno? Don't ever believe a word they say. They don't know their hind ends from a hole in the ground."

"Where were you when I was here before?"

"How would I know, you dimwit?" Jasper Jensen poked his head out and looked both ways. "Are you alone?"

Fargo pointed his Henry at the cluster of townspeople, barely visible. "Some of the folks from Inferno are with me."

"Are they, now?" Jensen said. "I told them and I told them but they wouldn't listen." He moved to one side. "Why don't you come in, and we'll jaw awhile? It appears I have some explainin' to do."

"Only for a minute," Fargo said, entering. He didn't want to leave the others out there too long. They must be wondering and worrying.

Jensen closed the door and indicated a chair. "Plant yourself, why don't you? I'm about to put coffee on."

Fargo set the Henry on the table. "We could all use some. And whatever you have for bandages."

"There it is again," Jensen said, moving to a cupboard.

"There what is?"

"They impose and they impose and they impose." Jensen opened the cupboard and reached in.

"It's not their fault some of them have been shot," Fargo said.

"Isn't it?" Jensen said, looking over his shoulder.

"Do you even know what's going on? Crillian has taken over the salt lick. He's demanding more money than you ever did. More than they can afford. They came here to try and take the salt lick back."

"It's not theirs to take."

"They've gone too long without salt. They're sick. Some are dying. They had to do something."

"They could leave."

Fargo wondered why the old man's hand was still in the cupboard. "Some have been shot. Their horses have been run off. They have to stand and fight."

"I didn't mean leave the lick, sonny boy," Jensen said. "They should have left Inferno when they had the chance. But they wouldn't listen."

"What are you talking about?"

Jensen took his hand from the cupboard. In it was an old Colt Dragoon, a heavy piece weighing over four pounds, with a seven and a half-inch barrel. To call it a cannon wouldn't be an exaggeration. It was already cocked.

"What the hell?" Fargo said.

"Give me an excuse, and I'll blow you to hell," Jasper Jensen said.

"I'm on your side."

"Hell, mister, you don't even know what my side is." Jensen came over, the Dragoon steady in his veined hand despite its weight.

"Enlighten me," Fargo said.

Jensen carefully reached across and pulled the Henry toward him. He leaned it against a chair and came around the table. "I'm helpin' myself to that six-shooter of yours. Be smart and stand there quiet-like."

"I want to help you against Crillian." Fargo sought to make himself plain.

"I don't need no help," Jensen said. "Especially since his side and my side are the same side." He moved behind Fargo, snatched the Colt, and set it on the chair the Henry was propped against. "Now then. Let's get to it."

"To what?" Fargo asked.

"To settin' you straight."

"The people outside—" Fargo began.

"Can rot in hell for all I care. I didn't want them to build a town. But they did anyhow. Even after I went to those who came first and told them to scat."

"What the hell is wrong with you?"

"Me?" Jensen said indignantly. "I'm not the one who imposes on folks. All I ever wanted was to be left alone but they wouldn't listen."

There was a light knock on the door and someone whispered, "Old man? You in there?"

"Him again," Jensen muttered. Moving wide of the table, he went to the door and opened it without looking. "Come on in."

Mayor Hoffstedder slipped inside, blinked several times on seeing Fargo, and quickly shut the door. "I wasn't about to without being asked. I know how grumpy you can be."

"He thinks he knows me," Jensen said to Fargo. "Him and his highfalutin airs. When I first went to him about gettin' rid of the town, he laughed in my face."

"Don't start with that again," Hoffstedder said. "I came to my senses, didn't I?"

"After I agreed to pay you three thousand dollars," Jensen said, moving back around the table.

Fargo was more confused than ever. "Where would you get that much money? Do you have it socked away?"

"I don't have a blamed cent to my name," Jasper Jensen said.

"What?" Mayor Hoffsteader said. "How do you expect to pay me the three thousand, then, damn you?"

"I don't," Jasper Jensen said. Picking up Fargo's Colt, he smiled at Hoffstedder and shot him in the face.

# 39

It happened so unexpectedly, Hoffstedder had no chance to defend himself or try to run. He crashed onto his back on the floor, convulsed, and went limp.

Jasper Jensen set Fargo's Colt back on the chair and pointed the Dragoon at Fargo. "I should do you, too, for sidin' with them."

"Old man," Fargo said, "you're plumb crazy."

"Like a fox," Jensen said, and tittered. "I've got 'em eatin' out of my hand and they don't know my hand is empty."

Blood was trickling down Hoffstedder's neck. His mouth was open, his tongue half-out.

"Tell me why," Fargo said, with a nod at the body.

"Why should I? You're nothin' to me except another damn nuisance I can do without."

"I've never done anything to you."

"You listen but you don't hear. The same as the folks in Inferno. They have ears but they're all plugged with wax."

"Make sense, damn you."

Jensen looked at the broken window and his brow puckered. "I just had me a thought. His runt might show up. I'd best do you in so I don't have to watch you and watch out for him, both."

"Runt?" Fargo said. "Do you mean Jaffer?"

"That's the one," Jensen said. "Hoffstedder's bodyguard. Hoffstedder hired him as insurance against me, was how he put it."

Fargo was desperately trying to understand. "If you and Hoffstedder were working together, why did he need to hire Jaffer to protect him from you?"

"You're not very bright, are you?" Jensen said. He motioned at the body. "You just saw me shoot him. He was the only one smart enough to savvy he couldn't trust me. I reckon he figured I'd sic Crillian on him."

"Why did you bring Crillian in? At least tell me that much."

"Dumb as hell," Jensen said, and shook his head in disgust. "It hasn't sunk in yet that I'm out to get rid of Inferno?"

"You want to destroy the whole town?"

Jensen muttered something. "You're commencin' to annoy me. Not *destroy*, you blamed jackass. I want the *people* out of there. I want them gone, for good. I want the town empty. Do you savvy now?"

"You want the town for yourself?"

"I swear," Jensen said. "You're stupider than cow shit. No, I don't want the damn town. As soon as they're gone, I'm burnin' it to the ground."

"You don't like towns?"

"I don't like people. I came out here pretty near twenty years ago to live by my lonesome. I toted wood and built my cabin. I have a spring, and critters come to drink and I shoot them for the meat. Deer and the like come to lick the salt, too. So I never want for vittles." Jensen sighed. "I was happy as could be until that damn town sprang up. I told them I didn't want them there but they wouldn't listen. They begged me to sell 'em salt so I did while I worked out how to get rid of them for good. Then I heard about Crillian, and told him I'd pay him a heap of money if he'd help me get rid of everyone in Inferno. I was thinkin' he'd shoot a few and the rest would scat. He had a better idea."

"The salt," Fargo said.

Jensen nodded. "He let them think he'd taken over the lick and told them they had to pay through the nose. They hummed and hawed and now look at them."

"All you wanted was for them to go?"

"How many times do I have to tell you same thing? Yes, yes, and yes. I want them gone. I want things to be like they were. I want there to just be me and no one else for a hundred miles around."

Fargo stared in amazement. "All of this, all these people dying, is because you want to be left alone?"

"Give yourself a pat on the back. You've finally figured it out. You have a brain the size of a pea but you do have one."

"You really are loco."

"A man is entitled to his privacy. I happen to like mine more than most. It's why I came so far out to live."

Rising anger smothered Fargo's astonishment. "The suffering those people have done. Women and kids as sick as dogs. All those who have died. So you can live as a damn hermit?"

"Simmer down, sonny. You'll bust a gut." The old man laughed. "You make it sound like it's wrong to want to be alone."

It took every iota of Fargo's self-control for him not to leap out of his chair and grab Jensen by the throat. "You miserable fool."

"I wouldn't call me names if I was you. I gave them fair warnin'. Pretty near talked myself blue in the face sayin' over and over that they should pack up and go. But would anyone listen? No. They poked fun at me and whispered behind my back. I took it as long as I could, and then I did what I had to."

"What about the women? The children?"

"Why do you keep bringin' them up? They're no different than the men. They're where they shouldn't be. But they won't be there for much longer. The ones who came here tonight will soon be dead. Those as stayed in town will have to leave or die without my salt." Jensen beamed happily. "At long last I'll be by myself again."

"Where do I fit in?"

"You don't," Jensen said. "That you're helpin' them is cause enough to splatter your brains." He raised his Dragoon. "I suppose I should get to it."

Gauging the distance between them, Fargo tensed. He couldn't possibly stop the old coot from shooting but he had to try.

"I bet you never thought this was how your life would end," Jensen said.

"Shoot straight, you bastard."

Jasper Jensen grinned. "I always do."

# 40

Sudden pounding on the front door caused Jensen to give a start. Scowling, he called out, "Who the hell is it?"

"Jasper?" Marshal Bubaker hollered. "Is that your voice we hear in there?"

"Hell," Jensen muttered. "Stay in that chair," he said to Fargo. "You move, you say a word you shouldn't, I'll put lead into him. Got me?"

"Jasper?" the lawman said again.

"Come on in, Marshal."

Bubaker strode in, and he wasn't alone. Behind him were Melissa Gebhart and the rest of the townsfolk. The lawman stopped cold at the sight of Hoffstedder's body. "What the hell? We heard a shot and I was worried something had happened to Fargo."

"Happened, hell," Jensen said, continuing to point the Dragoon. "It was him as shot poor Hoffstedder."

"I don't believe it," Melissa declared.

"I saw it with my own eyes, girl," Jensen said. "Hoffstedder accused him of bein' in cahoots with Crillian, and Fargo there up and shot him. I got the drop on Fargo and was makin' up my mind what to do when you folks showed up."

"I knew it all along," Parker said. "I knew he couldn't be trusted."

"This can't be," Bubaker said. He turned to Fargo. "Don't sit there like a bump on a log. Say something."

Fargo pointed a finger at the old man and shook his head.

"Why won't you talk?" Melissa asked. "What's going on?"

Just then a woman rushed in, pushing others out of her way. "They're coming!" she cried.

"Who?" Marshal Bubaker asked.

"Who do you think? That pack of killers. I heard them and saw them."

"Get everyone inside," the lawman said.

Jensen started around the table. "What? No. This is my home. You can't just barge in here and—"

He got no further. The survivors were anxiously pouring in, some helping the wounded. The first ones in had to move against the walls to make room for the rest. The cabin wasn't meant to hold nearly twenty people and it was a tight fit.

Within moments Fargo was surrounded. People were between Jensen and him, but the old man was glaring at him and might cut loose with that hand cannon if he tried anything.

"Didn't you hear me?" Jensen hollered at the others. "I don't want you in here."

Marshal Bubaker shouldered toward the window. "Ignatius Crillian is after us. We came out here to put an end to his extortion and he's nearly put an end to us."

"How is it you're still alive?" a man asked Jensen. "We'd heard Crillian had killed you."

"Don't believe everything you hear."

"That's no answer," Melissa said. "We're dying on your behalf. We deserve the truth. Why didn't you come to town so we could help you?"

"You're dyin' for *me*?" Jensen said.

"This is your lick. We thought he'd taken it from you. But here you are, big as life," Melissa said.

Bubaker took off his hat and carefully peered out. "I see them. They're moving around out there but I can't tell what they're up to." He motioned. "Someone douse that light."

"Hold on," Jensen said.

A townsman blew out the lantern, plunging the cabin into darkness.

Fargo sprang up and threaded toward the end of the table and the chair with his guns.

"I didn't want that light out," Jasper Jensen angrily declared. "You people just can't do what you want in a man's home."

"You haven't changed, have you?" Marshal Bubaker said from the window. "You're still as cantankerous as ever."

"We don't want Crillian's men shooting at us," Melissa said. "That lantern stays off."

"They're liable to shoot anyhow," Jensen said, his voice coming from a different spot.

"Why make it easier for them?" Melissa argued.

Fargo was almost around the table. A man was in his way, hunched over. "I have to get by," he whispered.

"Go to hell."

It was Parker.

Fargo resisted the temptation to knock him down. "Move, damn you," he whispered so Jensen wouldn't hear.

"Why are you talking like that?" Parker said. "Afraid of Crillian? Are you yellow as well as a turncoat?"

"If you don't get out of my way . . ." Fargo began.

A commotion broke out at the door. There was the thud of a blow and a gust of air filled the cabin.

"Stop him!"

The front door slammed and someone swore.

"What's going on over there?" Marshal Bubaker demanded. "Do I have to come over?"

"That old geezer," a man said. "He hit me and ran out."

"Why in hell would he do that?" Bubaker said. "Crillian will shoot him dead."

Fargo didn't need to keep quiet any longer. "Not when they've been working together this whole time."

"Why didn't you tell us that sooner?" Marshal Bubaker said. "What the hell got into you?"

"He was holding a gun on me. Or didn't you notice?" Fargo heard shouts outside. Jensen and Crillian reuniting, he figured. It wouldn't be long before Crillian peppered the cabin with lead or sought to drive them out. "For the last time," he said to Parker. "Move."

"Why don't you make me?"

"Fine," Fargo said. By now his eyes had adjusted enough that he could make out shapes and sizes. He let fly with an uppercut that caught Parker on the jaw. It about broke his hand and sent Parker crashing against others. In the ensuing confusion he barreled to the chair and quickly reclaimed the Colt and the Henry.

Marshal Bubaker had left the window and was trying to restore order. "What's going on? Let me through."

"I think it's Parker," a man said. "He's been knocked out."

"We need a light," a woman said.

"So Crillian can see inside and pick us off?" Bubaker said. "Use your heads." He reached those clustered around Parker. "Fargo? Is this your doing?"

"He was being a jackass again," Fargo said. He began to replace the cartridge Jensen had used to kill Hoffstedder.

"We need everyone able to fight. It could come at any moment."

"What could?" a woman asked.

Outside, the night erupted in gun blasts.

# 41

"Get down!" Fargo roared, and dived for the floor himself.

Pieces of glass left in the window broke and rained down. The door and the outside walls thudded to multiple impacts. A woman screamed and a man cursed.

Someone flattened next to Fargo and a hand fell on his shoulder. "They have us trapped," Melissa said. She sounded on the verge of panic.

"Stay calm," Fargo said. The walls were thick enough; no lead would get through. They only had to worry about the door and the window.

The shooting tapered, and in the lull a townsman bawled, "We can't stay in here. We'll die if we do."

"No one move," Marshal Bubaker said. "We're safe enough for the time being."

"Like hell we are," the man said, and rising, he darted to the door. "I'm not going to be picked off like a duck in a pond." He threw the door open and went to dash out.

More shots cracked.

The man in the doorway screamed as he was flung back inside and fell on top of others.

Jumping up, Fargo leaped over someone, slammed the door shut, and put his back to the wall.

A woman was weeping. A man uttered sounds remarkably like a fish out of water and thrashed violently.

"Who's been hit?" Marshal Bubaker asked. "How bad are they?"

It turned out that besides the dead man, three more were wounded. Two were minor wounds but the man thrashing on the floor had taken a slug in the chest and hadn't long to live.

"Horace was right," someone said. "We stay here and we're goners."

"Horace is dead," Marshal Bubaker said. "And you'll be dead, too, if you're as harebrained as he was."

Fargo risked a look out the window. Furtive figures were moving about. Crillian and his lead chuckers were up to something.

Melissa crawled over and rose and pressed against him. "I'm scared," she said in his ear. "So are a lot of others."

"Can't blame them." Fargo was more interested in what the hired assassins were up to.

"We could make a break for it," Melissa suggested. "All of us at once."

"We wouldn't get ten feet."

"As dark as it is, they'll be shooting blind. If we keep low and move fast, some of us can make it."

"Do you want to be one of those who doesn't?" Fargo saw more movement. Whatever the gun hands were doing, they were in a hurry about it.

Marshal Bubaker joined them. "This has gone from bad to worse. Everyone wants to light a shuck."

"Including me," Melissa said.

"I'm open to ideas," Bubaker told Fargo.

Over at the lean-to, an orange speck of light flared and grew into a tiny flame. A fire was being kindled. Fargo heard cracking and crunching and realized the lean-to was being torn apart for firewood.

"What are they up to?" Melissa wondered.

Hands and arms appeared, tossing bits and pieces of wood onto the growing fire.

"I could drop a few if they step into the light," Marshal Bubaker said.

"Don't waste the bullets," Melissa said.

Fargo raised the Henry. "I have some to spare." He fired twice at forms near the fire and they scattered.

In retaliation, shots came from all over, striking the cabin like hail.

"That sure riled them," Marshal Bubaker said, grinning.

The shooting didn't last long. When Fargo rose up for another look, the fire was blazing. A long piece of wood was thrust at it, a strip of cloth wrapped around the end.

The cloth burst into flame and the flame moved toward the cabin.

"God in heaven," Marshal Bubaker blurted. "They're not fixing to do what I think they're fixing to do."

Another makeshift torch was applied to the fire. When the cloth ignited, the man ran after the first.

"Oh no," Melissa breathed.

A man lying near them raised his head. "What's happening out there? Don't keep it a secret."

"I'm not sure yet," Bubaker said.

Fargo was. Crillian intended to set fire to the cabin.

Once more, Melissa pressed her lips to his ear. "We have to get everyone out of here before it's too late."

Fargo grasped her hand and moved to the door. "I'll go first to draw their fire. Once I have, you bring the rest. Make for the north end of the salt lick and then to the hills."

"I wouldn't know north from south," Melissa said.

"Bubaker will," Fargo hoped. He let go of her and gripped the latch while firming his hold on the Henry.

"Skye," she said, "please be careful."

At the rear of the cabin a woman said, "Does anyone hear that sound? Sort of like crackling?"

"I smell smoke!" a man exclaimed.

That was all it took. "The cabin is on fire!" someone bawled, and just like that, pandemonium was unleashed.

# 42

Fargo tried to stop the stampede by barring their way and shouting for them to calm down. He might as well have tried to stop a herd of terror-stricken buffalo. A man slammed into him, nearly knocking him down. Hands grabbed him and shoved him. He collided with Melissa and the two of them tottered back, off-balance.

"Don't panic, damn you!" Marshal Bubaker bellowed, to no avail.

The door was practically wrenched from its leather hinges and thrown wide open. A pair of men hurtled out, the rest streaming after them in a shoving, cursing, fear-filled mass.

That was when the shooting commenced. Shrieks and screams added to the bedlam.

Fargo could imagine the slaughter. He tried to stop those who hadn't gone through the door yet and was shoved a second time.

"Damn it, Allison, no!" Marshal Bubaker shouted, and tackled a woman about to run out.

A few more moments and the doorway was empty. The shots continued, though, and the screams.

Fargo moved to the window.

Bodies littered the ground. Some had gone right and some had gone left and others simply flew straight into the withering gunfire, and all had died. The barkeep, the clerks, the women, the wounded, were sprawled in heaps.

At his elbow Melissa burst into tears, turned away, and buried her face in her hands.

Marshal Bubaker pulled the woman he had saved to her feet and slammed the front door. She sobbed and buried her face in his shoulder. "It's all right, Allison," he said. She only sobbed louder.

"This is your fault, you son of a bitch," someone declared.

Fargo turned.

Parker hadn't fled. He was by the table, holding a revolver. "You did this to them. You tricked us into coming here and got them killed."

"He did no such thing," Marshal Bubaker said. "Put that six-gun down."

"Like hell I will," Parker said. "If I'd done this back in Inferno, all those people would be alive." He took a step and extended the revolver.

"No!" Melissa cried, moving between them.

"Out of the way, woman," Parker snapped. "I won't let you stop me. Your lover has this coming."

Fargo didn't know what made Melissa do what she did. Screeching like a bobcat, she threw herself at Parker. She swatted at his wrist and the six-gun went off, the slug plowing into the floor. Raking her fingers across his face, she drove him back against the table.

Parker swore furiously.

Fargo leaped to help. He tried to ram the Henry's stock into Parker's face but Melissa was in the way. Sidestepping, he drove the muzzle into Parker's ribs instead.

Parker bleated and doubled over. His six-gun went off again.

Melissa clutched herself and fell to her knees.

A red haze seemed to fill Fargo's vision. Gripping the Henry by the barrel, he swung it like a club. The stock caught Parker across the temple. Parker swore and sought to straighten, and Fargo swung again. Teeth crunched and blood spurted. Not holding back Fargo swung a third time and Parker let out a strangled whine and collapsed.

Fargo knelt next to Melissa. Her head was bowed and she was grimacing. Dreading the worst, he said, "Let me have a look."

She nodded without speaking.

Gingerly moving her hand, Fargo bent lower. The slug had seared her side, leaving a furrow that would scar. She was bleeding but not badly. "You'll live," he said.

Melissa looped her other arm over his shoulder and kissed him on the cheek. "I couldn't let him hurt you."

"That jackass," Marshal Bubaker said, coming over with the woman called Allison. "I should have left him in town."

"Forget Parker," Allison said. "I'm more worried about us. They'll finish us off now, won't they?"

"Who can say?" the lawman said.

Fargo moved to the window again. Seven or eight gun hands were moving among the bodies. Dreel was one of them. Ramirez another. Willy appeared and rolled a dead woman over with his foot.

Fargo was tempted to use the Henry but it might provoke them into rushing the cabin, and he had the others to think of.

Ramirez turned and hollered, "They're not all here, Señor Crillian."

"I don't see the scout or the tin star," Dreel said.

"Hunt cover," Crillian commanded.

The pack scattered.

Marshal Bubaker went to the rear of the cabin and roved back and forth, sniffing. "I don't hear the fire anymore," he informed them. "And the smoke's not as strong."

"It must have been a trick," Melissa said.

"To draw us out," Fargo agreed. He should have known Jensen wouldn't let his precious cabin be burned down.

"It worked," Marshal Bubaker said glumly.

They fell quiet until another shout from Ignatius Crillian reminded them of their plight. "I know you can hear me in there. How many of you are still alive?"

"Enough," Fargo responded.

"That you, scout?" Crillian said. "I suppose the marshal is still breathing, too."

"Him and ten others," Fargo said.

Crillian laughed. "Near as we can tell, there can't be more than four or five of you left."

"Step inside and we'll show you how many."

"I admire a gent who never gives up. I'm the same way. When I take a job, I always see it through."

"This one you won't," Fargo said.

"Let me guess. You're fixing to kill me and all of my men. Bluster doesn't become you."

"I don't have to do a thing," Fargo said. "Someone else will do it for me."

"I'll take the bait. Who?"

Fargo didn't answer. He was hoping Crillian would show himself. If he could drop him, the rest might skedaddle.

"What are you playing at?" Crillian hollered. "Who is going to stop me from killing you? I'd really like to know."

Again Fargo didn't respond.

"Being childish, are we?" Crillian waited, and when Fargo still didn't say anything, he shouted, "You and those with you have two minutes to come out with your hands over your heads or the killing commences."

Marshal Bubaker cupped a hand to his mouth. "Mister, you try to rush us, you'll lose an awful lot of men."

"That you, tin star?" Crillian said. "I've got news for you. You're already beat and don't know it." He paused. "Two minutes. I have my pocket watch out and I'm counting."

"He's bluffing," Bubaker said to Fargo. "Between the two of us, none of them will get in. We'll drop them as they come."

"I'll help, too," Melissa said.

Allison was worriedly wringing her hands. "We should run for it. They won't be expecting us to. We can get away."

"We wouldn't get any farther than the others did," the lawman said.

Allison glanced at the walls and the ceiling. "I don't like being cooped up." Tears trickled down her cheeks and she let out a low sob. "I don't want to die."

"Who does?" Bubaker said. He took her hand in his. "Don't dwell on it or you'll be of no use to us."

"I'm sorry," Allison said. "I can't help it."

Melissa moved to the table and came back with Parker's revolver. "This will come in handy."

"You use it," Fargo said. He had the Henry and his Colt.

"What do you figure they'll do? Attack all at once?"

Outside, Ignatius Crillian hollered, "One minute. Don't make it hard for me."

"Maybe we should do as he says," Allison said. "A bullet to the head is better than being beaten to death."

"Dead is dead," Marshal Bubaker said. "It doesn't matter how."

"It does to me," Allison said.

Fargo backed from the window. Melissa went with him. They stood where they could cover the door and the window, both. "Let them come," he said.

Marshal Bubaker pulled on Allison's arm. When she didn't move, he said, "Fargo has the right idea. Come on."

"I want to die quick," she said.

"Stop harping on that," Bubaker said. "Leave how it works out to the Almighty and help us fight them."

Allison took a deep breath, and nodded. "All right. I'll do as you want."

The lawman smiled and let go of her and came toward Fargo and Melissa.

Allison took a step, then whirled and darted to the door. Flinging it open, she ran out shouting, "Please don't shoot! Please don't shoot!"

Bubaker started after her but stopped at the boom of shots. "Not her, too," he said in horror.

"Why did she do that?" Melissa said. "She should have known."

"If it's the last thing I do," Bubaker said, "I'm going to kill Crillian." Shutting the door, he backed to where they were. "Now it's just the three of us."

"Parker is still alive," Melissa said.

"Who cares?" Bubaker said.

Fargo was listening for the commotion that would precede a rush. He heard Ignatius Crillian yell, "Now!"

Thunderous gunfire exploded, coming from the front and the sides of the cabin. The walls thudded. The door shook violently. Some of the shots came through the window but none hit them.

The firing went on and on. Finally Crillian yelled for it to stop.

In the quiet that ensued, Marshal Bubaker chuckled and said, "That didn't do them any good, did it? All they did was waste lead."

Behind them someone said, "I wouldn't say that, señor. Drop your guns, *por favor*, or die."

# 43

Marshal Bubaker spun, or tried to. A pistol cracked and he yipped in pain and his rifle clattered at his feet.

Fargo snapped his head around, and imitated stone.

Ramirez and Dreel were at the rear wall, Ramirez with a knife in each hand, Dreel with his pearl-handled pistols.

"Give me an excuse," Dreel snarled.

Melissa put a hand to her throat. "Dear God, no," she gasped. "How did they get in?"

"I will show you, señorita," Ramirez said. "But first, all of you will place your weapons on the floor."

Fargo would be damned if he would. He was sure he could put a slug into both before Dreel dropped him.

Then the front door crashed opened and in burst Willy and others. "Try anything and we gun you!"

Fargo couldn't drop all of them, not before they got him, and Melissa and Bubaker, as well. Fuming, he set his hardware down. Melissa hesitated, then did likewise. Marshal Bubaker had his left hand pressed to a wound in his right arm, which dripped blood.

"Well, now," Willy said, "that was as slick as anything."

Ramirez stepped to the lantern and presently the cabin filled with light. Turning, he pointed at a corner of the rear wall. "You wanted to know how, yes?"

A three-foot-square section of the wall had been pulled out and lay just outside, in the grass.

It was common practice for settlers to have a way to escape their cabin should they be set upon by hostiles or otherwise need to get out in a hurry. Some used trapdoors and a crawl space. Jasper Jensen had a bolt-hole.

"You didn't hear us open it with all the shootin'," Dreel crowed.

Grinning, Willy went to the window and hollered, "We have them, boss. And we didn't have to fire a shot."

In another minute in strode a smiling Ignatius Crillian. "Didn't I tell you that you wouldn't have to?"

"You're smart as anything, boss," Willy said in praise. "It's why I work for you."

"Why didn't you use that earlier?" Melissa asked with a nod at the bolt-hole. "You could have taken all of us by surprise instead of slaughtering everyone."

"Earlier would have been too soon," Crillian said. "There were too many of you in here and you were bound to spot what we were up to." He shook his head. "No, it was my ace in the hole, and I waited until it served me to best advantage. As for the slaughter, my employer was tired of trying to run all of you off. Killing you was perfectly fine with him."

"Jensen," Bubaker spat. "Where is that gob of spit?"

"Right here, tin star," Jasper Jensen said, entering. He was holding handfuls of coins and paper money and a few pokes. "I just got done going through the clothes of the folks lyin' out there."

"You robbed the dead?" Melissa said, aghast.

"They don't have any use for anything," Jensen said.

"You're the most despicable human being I've ever met."

Jasper Jensen snickered. "I never claimed to be a—what do they call it?—paragon of virtue."

"You're anything but," Marshal Bubaker said.

"Enough name-calling," Crillian interrupted. "Let's get this over with, Jensen, so my men and I can be paid and be on our way."

"I'm for that," Willy said.

"There're just these three," Crillian said. "Or do you want us to ride into Inferno and wipe out whoever is left there, as well?"

"Wipe them out or drive them out, it makes no never mind to me," Jensen said. "These three, though, deserve a dirt nap."

"Let me do it, boss," Dreel said eagerly.

Fargo was moments from breathing his last. All it would take was a nod from Crillian.

"I owe him," Willy said. "Let me put a slug or three into the son of a bitch, too."

It was said that when someone was on the verge of dying, they grasped at straws. Fargo grasped at one now. The only straw he had. He looked squarely at Ignatius Crillian and asked, "Has he paid you yet?"

"What?" Crillian said.

Jensen stiffened.

"Has Jasper Jensen paid you?" Fargo asked. "Do you and your men have the money he promised?"

"Five thousand dollars," Willy said, and chortled. "It's the most we've ever gotten for a job."

"You won't get it for this one," Fargo said.

"What are you on about?" Ignatius Crillian asked.

Uttering a bark of a laugh, Jasper Jensen said, "Don't listen to him. He's tryin' to stir up trouble."

"I didn't have to stir up any between you and Mayor Hoffstedder," Fargo said, nodding at the body. "You killed him anyway."

"What's this?" Crillian said. "Jensen told us you shot him."

"Hoffstedder was promised three thousand," Fargo said. "But Jensen doesn't have the money."

"He's lyin'," Jensen said.

Crillian turned toward him. "Is he? I get the feeling he's not."

"How can you take his word over mine? I paid you that two hundred you wanted up front, didn't I?"

"It's all the money we've seen," Crillian said.

"The rest will be paid when the job is done," Jensen said. "That was our deal, remember?"

Crillian stared thoughtfully at Fargo, then at the old man. "I'd like to see the rest of the money."

"You will when I pay you."

"Now," Crillian said.

"Not before any who are left in Inferno have been run off. That's the whole reason I hired you and your bunch."

"I took you at your word," Crillian said. "I'd hate to think you deceived me. This will end badly if you have."

"Do I strike you as dumb enough to try? What chance would I have against all of you?"

"I'd still like to see the money."

"It hurts my feelin's that you don't trust me," Jensen said.

"You'll be hurt a lot worse if you don't have it." Crillian gazed about the cabin. "Where do you have it hid?"

"Not where anyone can find it," Jensen said. "It's off in the lick, buried in the salt."

"Show me."

Jasper Jensen shook his head. "What's to stop you from shootin' me and takin' the money before the job is done?"

"I gave my word," Crillian said.

"I gave mine. And if it's not good enough for you, than yours ain't good enough for me." Jensen paused. "How about this. How about if I bring you half the money? You'll get the rest when the town is empty, as we agreed. Would that do?"

As they talked, Fargo had moved slightly so he was only a couple of steps from the lantern. Dreel and Ramirez and the others were so intent on their boss and Jensen that they didn't notice.

Crillian rubbed his chin. "I don't know."

"Showin' you half will prove the scout is blowin' smoke out his ass," Jensen said. "Maybe then you'll blow holes in his skull and put an end to him bein' a nuisance."

"Showing me half would prove Fargo is lying, all right," Crillian agreed. "How long will it take you to bring the money?"

"In the dark? Half an hour, I reckon."

"Take the lantern," Crillian said. "We don't need it."

"And have you see where I dig?" Jensen snorted and stepped to the door. "Make sure none of your boys follows me. I catch them, our deal is off, and you won't get another red cent."

Crillian didn't like that. "You don't tell me what to do, old man. I've put up with your cantankerous nature but don't press your luck. Fetch the money and be quick about it."

Muttering, Jasper Jensen walked out.

"You'll never set eyes on him again," Fargo predicted.

"I'd keep my mouth shut, were I you," Crillian said.

Dreel took a half step. "Let me plug him, boss. I'm itchin' to do him in."

"No."

"Why in hell not?"

Crillian moved to the window. "He might have done us a favor. If the old geezer is out to cheat us, we're not killing anyone else on his account."

"How about our own account? We owe the scout for Werner, remember? And the others he's shot."

"*Sí,*" Ramirez said. "He is too dangerous to let live."

"I'll do him," Willy offered.

Ignatius Crillian wheeled. With a calm that fooled no one because it was laced with menace, he said, "Since when do you question my judgment? Any of you? What I say goes. What I say *always* goes. Whoever has a problem with that, speak your piece."

No one said anything.

"I can't hear you," Crillian said, his hand resting on his revolver. "Speak up. Who here thinks they know better than I do?"

"Shucks, boss," Willy said. "We'd never buck you."

"I just want Fargo dead," Dreel said.

"Patience, gentlemen," Crillian said. "Bear with me a little longer, and you soon might get your wish."

"I hope so," Dreel said. "My trigger fingers are itchin'."

Fargo raised his arms and took a step back, which put him that much closer to the lantern. "Go easy on those triggers."

"Don't you worry," Dreel said. "It'll be when Mr. Crillian says I can and not before."

"We make a mistake, amigos," Ramirez said. "This one is too dangerous."

"You want something to do?" Ignatius Crillian said. "Go after the old man. Follow him. Find out where he has the money buried."

*"Sí, patrón,"* Ramirez said, and hurried from the cabin.

Fargo glanced at Melissa and then at Marshal Bubaker, trying to get their attention. She was staring morosely at the floor. The lawman was grimacing from his wound, his eyes half-closed.

"You have a reprieve, scout," Crillian said. "If Jensen is right and it's a trick, I'll have him skinned alive. I don't like being played for a fool. The last gent who did, I had his eyes gouged out and his tongue chopped off. Then I killed him."

Melissa roused to say, "You're despicable. Every last one of you."

"You ought to be nice to me, lady," Crillian said. "All I have to do is snap my fingers and my men will drag you out and take turns."

"Snap them, boss," Willy said, lustfully licking his lips. "I'd sure like to give her a poke."

Fargo's moment had come. Crillian and his gun hands were focused on Melissa. It was now or never.

He exploded into motion.

# 44

Taking a flying leap, Fargo kicked the lantern off the table. Simultaneously, a revolver cracked, the lead plucking at his sleeve. The lantern struck the wall and shattered, spewing flame and smoke. In the instant before the cabin plunged into darkness, the revolver cracked a second time. Fargo had crouched, and the lead whistled harmlessly above him.

"Don't shoot!" Crilliam bawled. "You might hit one of us."

Springing to Melissa, Fargo wrapped an arm around her waist and pulled her toward the bolt-hole. He reached out to grab Bubaker but the lawman wasn't there. A squawk and the sound of fists pounding flesh explained why. Bubaker had made a break for the front door.

Crouching, Fargo shoved Melissa through the hole and dived after her.

"Someone light a lucifer!" Crillian shouted.

"Where are they?" Willy cried.

His hand around Melissa's wrist, Fargo was up and running. He didn't know where he was going. He just ran. Any moment, he expected Creel or another gun hand to poke their head out of the bolt-hole and blast away.

"The marshal." Melissa recovered her wits. "We left him."

"Couldn't be helped."

Shouts broke out. A search would soon commence.

Fargo ran awhile, then hunkered. He needed some idea of where they were in relation to everything else. A check of the North Star told him they must be near the salt lick.

Torches flared near the cabin. Six, seven, eight of them. Those holding them fanned out.

"We can't stay in the open," Melissa whispered. "They'll find us."

Fargo moved toward the lick. He'd nearly forgotten about the pit and almost pitched into it before he realized the edge was right under his feet. The bottom was as black as a well.

"You're not thinking of going down in there, are you?" Melissa whispered apprehensively.

No, Fargo wasn't. The only way to reach the bottom was by an incline. The pit walls were six to eight feet high, and they'd be trapped.

Fargo turned to move along the rim and heard a noise. Bending, he peered over. Someone was down there. He heard the clink of metal and a swishing sound and realized someone was digging.

Melissa came to the same conclusion. "That must be Jasper Jensen down there, after his money," she said in his ear.

Fargo knew better. Jensen didn't have any. What was Jensen after, then? he wondered. "Come on," he whispered, and pulled her toward the incline.

"What are you doing?" Melissa demanded, digging in her heels. "We need to get out of here."

"We will." Fargo pulled harder.

"Consarn you, no," Melissa said.

Fargo took hold of her arm to haul her with him whether she wanted to come or not. An exclamation from the pit changed his mind. Jensen was talking to himself.

"Found it!"

Several grunts and plodding steps suggested the old man was coming up out of the pit.

Fargo flattened, yanking Melissa down with him. She didn't resist. A glance at their pursuers showed that the torches were nowhere near them.

Jasper Jensen lurched into view, carrying something heavy. A keg or a cask, from the looks of it.

"What is it he has?" Melissa whispered.

Jensen suddenly stopped and perked his head. "Who's there?" he demanded. "I know I heard someone."

Fargo almost swore. Melissa had given them away, but how was she to know the old buzzard could hear so well?

"Answer me, damn you," Jensen said.

To Fargo's surprise, a shadow detached itself from the bottom of the pit.

"It's only me, señor," Ramirez said.

"What are you doin' here, Mex?" Jensen snapped, easing his burden to the ground.

"Señor Crillian sent me to be sure you make it back," Ramirez glibly answered.

Unfolding, Jensen said, "How long were you hidin' there?"

"I merely keep an eye on you, señor." Ramirez came over. "This is the money, *sí*?"

"Look for yourself, you damn busybody."

Ramirez bent and put a hand on the keg. "This is familiar to me, señor."

"Good for you."

"What is in here?" Ramirez asked, giving the keg a shake.

"Your brains," Jasper Jensen said. His hand flicked to Ramirez's waist and rose.

Ramirez must have realized the same thing Fargo did, that the old man had drawn one of his knives, because Ramirez straightened and sprang back, or tried to.

Jensen buried the blade in Ramirez's throat. Not once but twice, tittering as he stabbed.

Melissa gasped.

Staggering, Ramirez made hideous gurgling sounds and clawed at his waist and his neck, both. He drew another knife but his legs buckled.

"Serves you right," Jasper Jensen said.

Ramirez cocked his arm to throw but he was terribly slow, so slow that Jensen had time to wrench on his forearm, making him drop the weapon.

"No, you don't, Mex."

"What do we do?" Melissa whispered.

Fargo wasn't about to do anything. The old man had that Colt Dragoon and he was unarmed. Besides which, the searchers were coming closer.

"I would have shot you but the others would hear," Jensen said to the still form at his feet. Picking up the keg, he stepped to the top of the pit and saw the torches. "What in hell is goin' on?"

One of the torches was almost to the lick.

Melissa dug her nails into Fargo. "What are you waiting for?"

Fargo rose and headed away.

Over at the cabin, Ignatius Crillian shouted, "Any sign of them yet?"

"Still lookin', boss," a searcher replied.

Fargo was confident that once they made it to the other side of the salt lick, they'd be safe. He tugged on Melissa's arm to hurry her and must have tugged too hard because she stumbled and grabbed him to keep from falling. She also sent a stone skittering over the edge.

The nearest man with a torch raised it aloft. "Over here!" he yelled. "I've found them."

# 45

Every time Fargo turned around, he was running for his life. He ran now, along the pit rim, pacing himself to match Melissa. She was doing her best but she was worn-out and huffed with every stride.

The next time Fargo looked back, the torches were bobbing and swaying to the running motion of their pursuers.

Melissa slowed, her hand to her ribs. "Sorry," she gasped. "It hurts so much."

Fargo scowled. They would be caught again, and he doubted he could escape a third time. Luck only went so far. He glanced into the pit. The bottom was about six feet down, and pitch-black.

Inspiration struck. Flinging one arm around Melissa, Fargo cupped the other to her mouth and propelled them over the brink. He braced his legs, hoping she had the sense to do the same. They came down hard and spilled onto their chests.

Melissa struggled and said something muffled by his hand.

"Hush!" Fargo growled in her ear.

Above them boots drummed. A torch appeared, and then another.

"Where the hell did they get to?"

"I don't know. But I'm sure they came this way."

"Let's keep goin'. If we don't find them, Crillian will be mad as hell. And you know how he gets when he's mad."

"There's nothin' they can do to stop us now."

"Do you want to tell that to Crillian?"

"No."

More arrived and together they jogged around the pit and off toward the looming hills.

Fargo didn't take his hand from Melissa's mouth until those who were after them were out of sight and out of hearing. "It's safe to talk."

"You should have warned me," Melissa said indignantly. "I was scared out of my wits."

"You're alive."

"That's not the point. Either of us could have broken a leg. Then where would we be?"

"Up a creek without a paddle." Fargo cautiously rose.

"What now? We make for town?"

"No." Fargo helped her up. "Be as quiet as you can."

"What are you up to now?" Melissa wanted to know. "I'd rather you don't spring another surprise on me."

Hugging the pit wall, Fargo headed for the incline that would take them out. "Crillian is the brains behind this bunch. We take care of him, the rest might skedaddle."

"By take care you mean kill."

"He's tried to do us in how many times now? Don't get squeamish on me."

"This might surprise you," Melissa whispered, "but I want him dead as much as you do. I want Jasper Jensen dead even more."

"He's on my list, too."

"What was that he was carrying? That keg or barrel?"

"I don't know," Fargo said, although he had a suspicion.

"Did you see him stab that Mexican? I always thought he was cantankerous but I was wrong. He's downright vicious."

Fargo was listening for sounds from above.

"We always knew he hated the town being there. I never imagined he'd go to such lengths to be rid of us."

"Some folks will stop at nothing to get what they want."

"But to let people suffer. Children, no less. To want to wipe them off the face of the earth. How can someone do that? How can he be so despicable?"

"The world isn't puppies and kittens," Fargo said.

"Yes, but to hurt people. I could never hurt another human being unless I'm forced to, like now."

"Other people aren't you."

"Is that all there is to it? Some of us are good and some of us are wicked? How can anyone want to be that way?"

"Melissa?"

"I know, I know. You're going to ask me to be quiet, or, knowing you, to shut the hell up."

"Took the words right out of my mouth."

From the vicinity of the hills came yells. The searchers were becoming frustrated. How long, Fargo wondered, before they backtracked to the pit? He picked up the pace.

Ramirez lay where he had fallen, his wide eyes glassy in the starlight.

Fargo was about to go around the body, but stopped. "I'll be damned." Jensen hadn't bothered to take Ramirez's knives or revolver. Quickly, Fargo helped himself to the six-shooter and a pair of blades. He gave another to Melissa, who dubiously hefted it.

"I've never stabbed anyone."

"It's easy. You stick them and get out of the way of the blood."

"If that was a joke it was in poor taste."

Fargo led her to where he could see the front of the cabin and the lean-to. Light spilled from the window and the open front door. At the edge of the light two figures were staring toward the torches and the hills.

Putting a finger to Melissa's lips, Fargo gestured to make it plain she should stay put. Flattening, he crawled.

Once again she didn't listen. She snaked after him, stopping when he stopped, moving when he moved.

Fargo drew close enough to recognize the two men, and hugged the dirt.

"They've lost 'em, boss," Dreel said. "They're comin' back."

Crillian had his hands on his hips and was tapping a boot. "Where did Jensen get to? He should have been back with the money by now."

"That old buzzard probably has it buried ten feet deep," Dreel said. "Don't worry. Ramirez won't let him pull anything on us."

"It's the scout who worries me."

"He's just one hombre," Dreel said. "I set eyes on him again, he's as good as dead."

"I never should have taken this job," Crillian remarked. "It's not the usual work we do."

"We're guns for hire. We can't be choosy."

As if he hadn't heard, Crillian went on. "One thing has bothered me about this from the start. The old man claims he heard about me from someone who was passing through."

"So?"

"So you saw how he is. Jensen hates people. Hates them worse than anything. Hates them so much, he'd wipe out an entire town."

"So?" Dreel said again.

"Only those on the shady side of the law know about us.

Which has me wondering what Jasper Jensen did before he came here, and even if that's his real handle."

"What are you sayin'? That he's lied to us from the start? That Jensen might not even be his name?"

"I'm remembering someone I heard about years ago. In Missouri, it was. A lunatic, they called him, who went on a killing spree. Men. Women. You name it. They never caught him."

"Jensen does have spooky eyes," Dreel said. "One look and you can tell he's not all there."

"Once he shows up with the money, we'll pay the town a visit," Crillian said. "Mostly women and children are left. It should be easy to drive them out. After that, he can set his fires and it'll be over."

"Jensen plans to burn the town down?"

"Every last building."

"I never heard the like." Dreel placed his hands on his revolvers. "Before we can go anywhere, we have to find and kill the scout and that gal he's with."

"We certainly do," Crillian said. "I don't want to be looking over my shoulder the rest of my days. No matter what, Fargo has to die."

"Consider it done," Dreel said.

# 46

The searchers returned. Some of their torches had gone out, others flickered on the verge.

Willy was among them and reported, "We lost them, Mr. Crillian. I'm awful sorry."

"That damn scout is tricky," another said.

"By now he's probably on his way to Inferno," Ignatius Crillian declared. "Hopefully, we've seen the last of him."

Dreel was more concerned about something else. "Did any of you see any sign of Ramirez and that old man out there?"

"Sure didn't," Willy said. "Shouldn't they have been back by now?"

Crillian motioned. "Let's go inside. We'll give them a little longer and then all of us will go looking."

"I could use some coffee," Willy said. "All this runnin' around has me tuckered out."

"I could use some myself," Crillian said.

They filed inside but left the cabin door open. It surprised Fargo that they didn't leave someone to stand guard. Crillian wasn't usually so careless.

"What do we do?" Melissa whispered.

Fargo would like to look for the Ovaro, but just then a two-legged figure hastened from behind the lean-to toward the cabin. By the way it was stooped over and its shuffling gait, it could only be one person.

Melissa saw it, too. "Why, that's Jasper Jensen. What's he doing?"

Jensen made it to the far side of the cabin undetected by those inside and slipped out of sight.

A presentiment filled Fargo. He remembered the heavy keg and what Ramirez had said. Grasping Melissa's arm, he whispered, "We have to get as far away as we can."

"Why? Jensen didn't see us."

"Don't argue for once." Hauling her upright, Fargo jogged to the southeast. Eventually it would bring them to the road.

They hadn't gone but a short way when a racket at the cabin brought him to a stop.

Harsh yells were punctuated by the blast of pistols. Jensen reappeared, running for his life, as out the front door spilled Crillian and Dreel and others. More came from around the side.

"What in the world?" Melissa exclaimed.

"They caught him setting the black powder," Fargo guessed, pulling her down once more so they wouldn't be spotted.

"Jensen was going to blow them up?"

"He doesn't have the money to pay them. He has to do something or they'll kill him."

"They'll kill him anyway, now."

A couple of gun sharks hastened into the dark and came back leading horses. Everyone mounted. Crillian at their head, they rode hard after the man who had hired them.

That left the cabin deserted and empty.

"I wonder," Fargo said to himself. "Stay here." He broke into a run.

By now it was predictable. Melissa stayed at his side, asking, "Why are we going to the cabin?"

"My guns," Fargo said. That was where he'd last seen them. It might be too much to expect they were still there but he had to look.

"I'm getting a cramp from all this running."

"Next time I tell you to stay put, stay the hell put."

"Has anyone ever told you that you can be mean at times?"

"Melissa, damn it."

"Bossy, too."

A coffeepot was perking and the aroma had filled the cabin. On the table lay a pile of weapons confiscated from the townsfolk. The gleam of brass gave the Henry away. The Colt was near the bottom with other six-shooters. Even better, over on the counter was his hat.

"You look happy," Melissa remarked.

Fargo was. He checked that the Colt was still loaded and twirled it into his holster. The Henry molded to his hands as if part of him. "Pick a rifle and revolver." While she did, he went to the door and watched.

"I found the ones I was using. What next?"

Fargo went around to the side. Jensen had started to dig a hole to place the keg in. Why he hadn't simply set it next to the wall and lit the fuse he'd rigged from a strip of cloth, Fargo didn't know.

"Is that enough powder to blow the cabin up?" Melissa asked.

"Let's find out." Fargo ran back inside. The lucifers were still there. He brought several out and squatted by the keg. "When I say to, we run like hell."

"I should say you shouldn't. I should say it's wrong to blow a man's home up. But God help me, I won't. A lot of good people are dead because of him. You have my consent and my blessing to blow it to hell."

"You done?"

"There you go, being mean again."

Fargo struck a lucifer, applied it to the cloth, and sprinted to the south as if his buckskins were on fire. When he looked back, the strip was sputtering. He slowed, thinking he might have to relight it, but larger flames flared, moving up the strip with startling speed. He ran for all he was worth.

Melissa was hard on his heels, sounding like a steam engine. "I am so tired of running," she complained.

The explosion was spectacular; a blast so tremendous, it seemed to shake the sky. The cabin wall and most of the roof were obliterated in a shower of broken pieces and bits.

Fargo was buffeted as if by a strong wind. He slowed, and grinned. The last section of roof was collapsing, sheets of fire spewing coils of smoke, and the flames were spreading. In half an hour there wouldn't be anything left.

"Oh my," Melissa said, and giggled.

Their elation was short-lived.

Hooves pounded, alerting them that the killers for hire were coming back.

# 47

Crillian had sent Willy and two others. They galloped to the cabin, or as close as they dared approach the raging flames.

"Son of a bitch!" Willy exclaimed. "Who could have done that?"

"Maybe the old bastard lit the powder and we didn't realize it," one of his companions said.

"And it took this long to go off?" Willy scoffed.

Fargo turned and scuttled toward them. He must be quick or they would spot him.

"You see anyone?" Willy said, rising in the stirrups.

"Nobody," the third man said. "Let's catch up to the rest." He raised his reins to ride off.

"Not so fast," Willy said. "We should try to find who did this. If we don't, Mr. Crillian will be upset."

"Who's going to tell him we didn't?" the third man asked.

"I will," Fargo said, stepping out of the shadows with his Henry to his shoulder. For several heartbeats they were rooted in consternation. Then one stabbed for his six-shooter with a cry of, "It's the scout!"

Fargo shot him in the chest, worked the lever, and shot the second man as the gun hand unlimbered his six-gun. That left Willy, who gamely jerked his hogleg and pointed it just as Fargo cored his elbow. Willy screamed, his revolver dropped, and he attempted to rein around.

Darting in front of Willy's mount, Fargo said, "Try and you die."

Willy thrust his good arm at the stars. "Don't shoot," he cried. "I'll do anything you say."

"Where's Crillian?"

"After the old man," Willy answered. "Jensen tried to blow us up. He had a horse hid and lit a shuck for Inferno, and Mr. Crillian said he'd chase him clear to hell if he had to."

Melissa ran up and pointed her rifle at Willy. "Want me to shoot him?"

"Collect the other horses," Fargo said. "Willy goes with us."

"What do we need him for?" Melissa said. "He'll turn on us the first chance he gets."

"Crillian sent three men to investigate the explosion," Fargo said. "He'll expect three men to return."

Melissa looked down at herself. "I'm not male but I suppose I can pass for one in the dark."

"You won't have to," Fargo said, and didn't elaborate. "Now how about those horses?"

"Sure thing." Melissa departed at a fast clip.

Almost immediately, Willy groaned and doubled over as if he were in pain. "I can't go anywhere unless you bandage me."

"Put a finger in the bullet hole," Fargo said.

"I'll bleed to death before we catch up!" Willy squealed. "It will only be the two of you and Mr. Crillian will be suspicious."

"I'll prop you in your saddle."

"You have an answer for everything," Willy complained. "But wait and see. You won't pull the wool over Mr. Crillian's eyes."

Melissa took longer than Fargo liked. One of the horses wouldn't let her get near it. She had to coax and soothe it, and even then, time and time again it ran off. Finally she succeeded.

By then the cabin was fully engulfed, the flames searing fifty feet into the air, the crackle and pop of wood constant.

"If Jasper Jensen ever finds out what you did," Willy remarked, "he'll skin you alive. He liked that cabin. It took him months to haul the wood from the mountains."

"Your boss will likely take care of him before I can," Fargo said.

"Depends on if the old coot reaches town. There are plenty of places for him to hide. It could take a while to root him out."

"There's irony for you," Melissa said.

"There's what?" Willy asked.

"Never mind," Fargo said. "Head out. If you get a notion into your head to make a break for it, remember we're right behind you."

"You'd shoot a man in the back?"

"Wouldn't you?" Fargo said, trying to recollect if he ever had.

"Hell," Willy muttered.

On reaching the road they headed east. Willy behaved, and as they neared the hills, a large animal with white patches came trotting toward them.

It was the Ovaro.

In his elation, Fargo forgot himself and moved ahead of Willy to reach the stallion that much sooner. Swinging down, he patted the stallion's neck. "I wondered where you got to, big fella."

Riding up, Willy said, "Give it a kiss, why don't you?"

Fargo shoved the Henry into the scabbard and stepped into the stirrups.

Willy leaned on his saddle horn. "We should rest. I feel weak from all the blood I've lost."

"We're not stopping," Fargo said, setting him straight. "You'll just have to be careful you don't fall off and break your fool neck."

"Not that you would give a damn."

"I'd laugh," Fargo said.

"God, I hate you."

After that they rode in silence.

Fargo held to a walk. They had five miles to cover. He saw no need to tire the horses more than he had to. And so long as the townsfolk stayed indoors, they should be safe enough from Jasper Jensen. The old man would have his hands full eluding Crillian.

When they were only about a quarter mile out, Melissa brought her horse alongside the Ovaro. "There're not many lights."

"At this time of night there should hardly be any," Fargo said.

"Shows how much you know. The families of those who went to the lick should be up waiting for them to come back. There should be more lights than we see."

"Maybe they don't want to draw attention to themselves."

"I suppose," Melissa said.

They were almost in rifle range when Fargo had Willy draw rein. He counted only three lit windows, one of which was likely the saloon. The main street, what he could see of it, appeared to be empty.

"How do we handle this?" Melissa asked.

"*We* don't," Fargo said. "You're to stay with him. If he acts up, shoot him in the gut."

"Bastard," Willy said.

"I live there," Melissa said. "Those are my friends. I should go with you. I've proven I can take care of myself, haven't I?"

Fargo was truthful with her. "You'd hinder me." He couldn't watch out for her and him, both. To Willy he said, "How many are with Crillian?"

"I'll never tell."

"You will if I shoot you in the knee."

"Seven," Willy said.

Fargo shifted in the saddle and smiled at Melissa Gebhart. "For once listen to me."

"If you insist. But I don't like it." Melissa bobbed her chin at Inferno. "What are you going to do once you get there?"

"Kill everybody," Fargo said.

# 48

Except for the lights, Inferno might as well have been a ghost town. Nothing moved. No sounds broke the stillness.

Hidden in a well of shadow at the end of Main Street, Fargo sought some sign of the guns for hire and the horses they'd ridden in on. He figured that Crillian would conduct the hunt for Jensen on foot.

Alighting, Fargo led the Ovaro to a house with a fence and tied it well back from the street. Shucking the Henry, he commenced a hunt of his own.

He had been right about the saloon. Light streamed from the front window.

Hugging the buildings, he reached it and peered in.

No one was there. Half-empty bottles lined the bar. Several broken ones littered the floor and a table had been overturned.

Fargo turned and went to the rear. The back door was ajar. Pushing it with his boot, he eased inside. A short hall brought him to the front. He saw no one. Ducking, he darted behind the bar, helped himself to a bottle of Monongahela, and hunkered. "Damn, I need this." He opened it, took a long swig, wiped his mouth with his sleeve, and smiled.

Over near the batwings, something crunched.

Fargo mentally cursed himself for being a jackass. There must have been someone there all along. He set down the bottle and pivoted to dart to the hall. Voices gave him pause.

"The boss will be mad if he catches us."

"He's at the other end of town."

"I still don't like it. You can go without for a while yet."

"No I can't. It's Crillian's own fault. He let us have a taste and then made us go look for that old bag of bones. I want more than a taste."

"Be quick about it, Stiles."

Fargo could see them in the mirror but they didn't spot him. They came to the middle of the bar. The one who must be Stiles helped himself to a bottle, and chugged. His pard kept glancing at the window.

"Hurry it up, damn you."

"You worry too much."

Avoiding pieces of glass, Fargo crabbed to the end of the bar but didn't show himself yet.

"That old bastard could be anywhere," the other gunman said. "We might never find him."

"Hell," Stiles said, "he'd be dumb as a stump to stick around, knowin' we'd be after him." He chugged more whiskey.

Fargo quietly leaned the Henry against the bar. Loosening his Colt in its holster, he stepped out. "Gents," he said.

Stiles gaped with the bottle half-raised. His friend spun. Neither resorted to their hardware.

"What the hell?" the pard said.

"Anytime you're ready," Fargo told them.

"What is this?" Stiles said. "Are you fixin' to bed us down, permanent?"

"I am."

"Because of the ruckus at the salt lick? Hell, we've forgotten all about that. You should scat while you can."

"You and your friends tried to kill me. I don't forget a thing like that."

Stiles smirked at his partner. "What was that I just said about dumb as a stump? Here's another one." He set the bottle down. "We're not green behind the ears, mister."

"Prove it," Fargo said.

Stiles shifted and, in doing so, blocked Fargo's view of his partner. Simultaneously, he stabbed for his six-gun.

With a flick of his wrist, Fargo had his Colt out. He fanned a shot into Stiles, fanned another as the pard sprang clear to get off a shot of his own. The partner twisted half-around and cried out. Fargo fanned again, drilling Stiles a second time. The pard attempted to aim, his teeth bared, and Fargo sent a slug into his mouth

Both men had been shot twice and were oozing to the floor. Stiles managed to squeeze trigger and hit the bar.

Fargo shot him in the forehead.

Swiftly reloading, he scooped up the Henry and ran down the hall to the back door. Crillian was bound to investigate.

In a lapse of caution, Fargo bounded into the night without looking. He hadn't taken two steps when his arm was seized. Instinctively, he went to point the Henry. "You!" he blurted.

"Me," Marshal Bubaker said, looking the worse for wear. His shoulder was bandaged but so crudely done, he must have bandaged it himself. "I was sneaking by and heard the shots."

"Crillian has two less gun sharks," Fargo informed him. "We have to make ourselves scarce."

"Follow me. I know this town like I do the back of my own hand."

A minute later they were crouched in a toolshed that fringed a house with a small withered garden.

"No one is after us yet," Bubaker said, his eye to a crack in the door.

"I'm glad you're still breathing."

"I have you to thank," Bubaker said. "When you lit out that hole in the cabin wall with Miss Gebhart, all of them but one went after you. He must have figured I was too hurt to do anything because he stood looking out the window, so I conked him over the noggin and skedaddled. Found a horse and here I am. Got into town about five minutes ago."

"We didn't see you on our way in."

"I circled to the north," Bubaker said. "Reckoned I'd be less likely to be spotted." He paused. "By 'we' do you mean Miss Gebhart is still alive, too?"

"She is," Fargo confirmed. "Keeping watch over Willy."

"I'm right pleased to hear it. I like that gal." The lawman bent to the crack and gave a start. "Uh-oh."

"What?" Fargo couldn't see past him.

"Here they come," Bubaker said. "Looks like the whole pack. The big man himself is leading them. And there's that Dreel."

"Time to swap more lead," Fargo said.

# 49

"They're going into the saloon," Marshal Bubaker reported.

"Let me have a look." Fargo was just in time to see the last of them go in. "They'll be back out after us in no time," he predicted.

"There're only six now, counting Crillian. Too bad I don't have a smoke wagon.

Fargo glanced at the lawman's holster. He hadn't noticed it was empty.

"Take my revolver."

"If we can make it to my office, I have a spare six-shooter in my desk drawer and a shotgun in the gun cabinet."

"Until then," Fargo said, sliding his Colt out and shoving it at him, "use this."

"I'd rather borrow your rifle."

"With your shoulder as it is?"

"To tell the truth, I'm not much of a pistol shot. With a rifle I can usually hit what I aim at."

"Suit yourself," Fargo said, and handed the Henry over.

"I'm obliged." Bubaker ran his hand over the brass receiver. "I've never shot one of these but I've always wanted to. It's about the prettiest rifle I ever did see. How many cartridges does it hold?"

"There are sixteen in the magazine and one in the chamber," Fargo informed him.

"Lord Almighty. I can shoot all blamed week."

Fargo pushed the shed door open. "Get set. As soon as they show themselves, we'll shoot them to ribbons."

"An hombre after my own heart," the lawman said.

Weapons trained, they waited. Minutes drifted by, and Crillian and his men didn't reappear.

"Maybe they decided to have a few drinks," Bubaker speculated.

"I'll go have a look-see. Wait here."

"Not on your life. I owe it to the folks who died out at the lick tonight to see that justice is done."

Fargo moved quickly to forestall being caught in the open. A peek down the hall puzzled him. He didn't hear or see anyone.

"Where'd they get to?"

Cocking the Colt, Fargo sidled inside. The bodies were where they had fallen, in a spreading scarlet pool. Not a trace, though, of Ignatius Crillian and his gun hands.

"Don't this beat all," Bubaker said. "They must have gone out the front."

Fargo wasn't so sure. His instincts warned him not to show himself, that something wasn't right.

"What are you waiting for?" the lawman asked, and brushed past him. "We can take them by surprise."

"Good idea," someone said, and from behind the bar rose Ignatius Crillian and three others, their firearms leveled. The next instant Dreel and some others burst in through the batwings.

Marshal Bubaker stopped, the Henry pointing at the floor. "Hell in a basket."

"Not very prudent of you," Crillian said. "Drop that rifle and have the scout step out where we can see him."

"How did you know we were after you?" the lawman asked.

"How stupid do you think I am?" Crillian rejoined. "Whoever killed Stiles and Benjamin was bound to be in the vicinity. So I set a little trap."

"Clever of you."

"You heard Mr. Crillian," Dreel snapped. "Drop that rifle or there'll be hell to pay."

Fargo took a page from Crillian's book. Grabbing Bubaker by the back of his collar, he shoved him down the hall even as he squeezed off shots at the men at the bar and at Dreel. Crillian ducked from sight. Dreel fanned two shots that struck the jamb.

"Run like hell," Fargo urged Bubaker. He fired again to discourage pursuit and, with lead thudding into the walls, raced after the lawman.

"This way," Bubaker hollered as they sped into the night. He flew past the next building and around to the side.

Fargo reloaded as they went. He figured the tin star would stop at Main Street and look before committing himself, but Bubaker barreled out and across heedless of the danger.

A rifle cracked. A lone shooter was in front of the saloon.

Fargo fired on the fly and the man retreated through the batwings. Bubaker entered an alley. Fargo was watching behind them and didn't pay much attention until he collided with a wheelbarrow, of all things. He and it crashed to earth. His chin hit so hard, it was a wonder he had any teeth. Scrambling up, he leaped over it.

"That was clumsy," Bubaker said. "Hurry!"

Fargo looked back. The shooter from the saloon was in the alley mouth. They fired at the selfsame moment and the man skipped out of sight.

Bubaker turned left.

Fargo did the same, and had to dig in his bootheels to keep from smashing into him. The lawman had stopped and was doubled over, taking deep breaths.

"Sorry," he wheezed. "It's the wound. I was weak enough from not having enough salt all these weeks, and now this."

No one charged out of the alley after them. Crillian was shouting something that Fargo couldn't make out. He replaced the spent cartridge, saying, "We don't have all night."

"Give me another minute," Bubaker said. He added, "I know a good place to hide."

"Hide, hell," Fargo said. He was tired of running. "It's them or us."

"There are too many. We should whittle them down first."

"You can whittle all you want," Fargo said. Reentering the alley, he warily advanced. He didn't particularly want company but he got it anyway.

"Are you trying to get yourself killed?" Fresh blood stained Bubaker's bandage and sweat dotted his pasty face.

"I can go it alone."

"Why not make them come to us? That would be smarter."
"Do you see them coming?"
Bubaker shook his head. "That one must have gone to tell Crillian where we got to."
"I'll show myself so they concentrate on me," Fargo said. "You stay in the alley. When the shooting starts, pick off as many as you can."
"That's the best you can come up with?"
Before Fargo could answer, Ignatius Crillian shouted from over near the saloon.
"Scout! I have a surprise for you! Come on out! I give you my word we won't shoot."
"I don't like the sound of that," Marshal Bubaker said. "It could be a trick."
"Scout? Did you hear me?" Crillian yelled. "Don't keep me waiting. She'll pay if you do."
"She?" Marshal Bubaker said.
A sinking feeling in his gut, Fargo reached Main Street and risked a quick look.
He had a hunch what he would see and hoped he was wrong, but he wasn't. "They have Melissa."

## 50

Melissa Gebhart stood straight and defiant in the center of the street. Her fists were clenched and she was glaring at her captors, who had ranged on either side of her and trained their guns. A gash on her temple was bleeding.
Willy, grinning savagely, had hold of her arm.
Crillian and Dreel were under the saloon overhang, Crillian the portrait of confidence, Dreel with his hands on his pearl-handled revolvers.
"Fargo!" the former shouted. "No more cat and mouse. Show yourself or the woman takes one in the leg."

"Be ready," Fargo said to the lawman, and strode into the open, the Colt low at his side.

None of the gunmen covered him. They kept their weapons pointed at Melissa Gebhart.

"About time," Crillian said. "I was beginning to think you must have a yellow streak."

Fargo bobbed his head at Melissa. "You're a fine one to talk, you son of a bitch."

"She's a means to an end," Crillian said. "The end being the end of you."

Melissa tried to take a step but Willy jerked her back. "I'm sorry," she said. "I was careless and this jackass jumped me."

"Jackass, am I?" Willy said, and slapped her.

Melissa barely flinched. A drop of blood trickled from the corner of her mouth as she gave Willy a withering look of pure scorn.

"I didn't tell you to hit her, William," Crillian said.

"She insulted me."

"I'll do a lot worse should you hit her again."

Out of the corner of his eye, Fargo saw that Marshal Bubaker had stretched out on his belly and taken aim with the Henry. None of the hired guns had noticed him yet. To keep them distracted he said, "Let her go. I'm out in the open where you wanted me. You don't need her anymore."

"Were I a man of principle, I'd agree," Crillian said. "Since I'm not, she stays. And if you don't do exactly as I say, William there will blow her guts out her spine."

"Gladly," Willy said.

Fargo set himself. But first he asked, "Did you ever find Jensen?"

"Not yet. When I do, he'll wish he never tried to use me."

"I'll have to finish it, then," Fargo said.

Ignatius Crillian laughed. "I admire a gent with confidence. I have a lot of it, myself."

"You'll need it."

Dreel stepped from under the overhang. "Let me do it, boss. I'm tired of him and his mouth."

"Why not?" Crillian said. "With him out of the way, we can wrap this up." He motioned. "Be my guest."

"About time, by God." Sneering at Fargo, Dreel sauntered to the middle of the street. He inadvertently put himself between Fargo and Willy, who moved a few steps to one side to see better.

"It's just you and me now, scout," Dreel said. "No one will butt in. I give you my word."

"Which isn't worth a gob of spit," Fargo said.

Dreel surprised him by not losing his temper. "I'll say one thing for you, mister. You're the sneakiest cuss I've ever run across. You gave us a good run out at the salt lick."

"I try my best."

"Yes, sir," Dreel said. "You're bein' sneaky right now. Or did you think I wouldn't see that you're holdin' your six-shooter down by your leg?"

"Good eyes," Fargo said.

"Put it in your holster," Dreel said. "Nice and slow. You don't, and Willy shoots your gal friend."

"I'll send her to hell," Willy said.

Fargo didn't hesitate. The slight edge having the Colt out gave him wasn't worth her life. He slowly raised the Colt to his holster, dipped the barrel in, and let it come to rest. "Happy now?"

"I want it fair," Dreel said.

"Is that what you call using her against me?"

"That was Mr. Crillian's doin', not mine," Dreel said. "I like to go at someone head on. I like to see the look in their eyes when I gun them."

"You would."

"There you go again. But it won't work. I'm an old hand at this. You can't afford a temper in a gunfight. It can get you killed."

"I never would have taken you for having brains."

Dreel snorted. "You never stop, do you?" He lowered his hands to his sides and rolled his shoulders, relaxing them. "You'll make my sixteenth, by the way."

"You count them?" Fargo said.

"Everybody does. Some gents like to count all the money they have. Some count the women they've bedded. Men like us, we count how many we've bucked out in blood."

"Don't lump me with you," Fargo said. "I never think about them again if I can help it. It happens and it's over and that's it."

"I aim to hit fifty before I'm through."

"Is that all?" Fargo taunted.

"Listen to you," Dreel said.

Ignatius Crillian moved from under the overhang, too. "What is this? Are you two going to stand there jawing all day?"

"I was leadin' up to it," Dreel said.

"Leading, hell," Crillian said. "I thought Willy liked to talk a lot but you have him beat."

A flush of anger spread up Dreel's face. "You've no call to treat me like I'm no-account. I've never let you down, have I?"

"To your credit, you haven't, no."

"I'm not Willy."

"Hey now," Willy said.

Crillian gestured. "I have places to be, things to do. As soon as you're done with him, we'll find Jensen and finish this and head to Denver so I can recruit replacements for the men I've lost. Now get to it or the rest of us will do it for you."

Dreel locked eyes with Fargo. "You heard the man."

"I did."

"Anytime you're ready."

"You think you're that good?"

"I know I am."

"Damn it to hell," Crillian growled.

"One thing," Fargo said to Dreel.

"Eh?"

"I know Ramirez was your pard."

"What about him?"

"Jasper Jensen killed him. I saw it. He stabbed Ramirez in the throat. Never gave him a chance."

Dreel did the last thing he should have done. He blinked.

# 51

When a man was out to kill you, any edge helped—a lesson Fargo had learned the hard way. Whether it was a shooting affray, as they were sometimes called, a knife fight, or a slugging match with fists, the slightest advantage could mean the difference between an early grave and living to admire the next sunset.

Fargo had seen Dreel draw. The gun hand was ungodly quick.

So if Fargo could spoil Dreel's concentration and slow him for a fraction of a second, all the better.

Fargo had reckoned that mentioning Ramirez might do it. Dreel would be thinking of his friend and not his pistols.

The instant Dreel blinked, Fargo drew. Dreel's own hands flashed and they both fired but Fargo's was a heartbeat sooner. The slug cored Dreel's chest. Fargo felt a pluck at his sleeve and fanned a second shot, aiming higher this time. A hole appeared in Dreel's left cheek and the back of his head exploded in a shower of gore. It happened so fast, the others were caught flat-footed.

Willy's mouth fell open in surprise, and Fargo sent a slug through it. He heard the Henry boom and another of the gang fell. Then everyone was shooting at once. He saw Melissa throw herself flat. He needed to hunt cover, too. Flying toward a horse trough, he fired as he went. He reached it and dived over.

His fingers flying, Fargo reloaded. The Henry was blasting and revolvers in the street cracked.

Above it all rose a roar from Ignatius Crillian. "Kill them, damn your hides!"

Fargo finished and pushed up to his knees. He aimed at Crillian, who had backed to the batwings, but had to drop down when lead thwacked the trough.

"I'm hit!" a man cried.

Fargo pushed up again. Crillian had disappeared. Only two gunmen were still on their feet and they were retreating down the street, shooting. A third man, scarlet staining his shirt, had fallen to one knee and was gamely exchanging shots with Marshal Bubaker. Fargo sent lead into his head.

Melissa had thrown her arms protectively over hers. She looked at Fargo and at the saloon, and pointed. "Look out!" she screamed.

Crillian was in the window, taking aim.

Rolling under a hitch rail, Fargo jackknifed onto the boardwalk and pressed his back to the wall. He wondered why Crillian hadn't fired and glanced at Melissa, who shook her head.

"I don't see him," she said.

Fargo sprang to a gap between the buildings and ran to the rear, reaching it just as Crillian burst out the back door of the saloon. Crillian was looking behind him, down the hall.

"Surprise," Fargo said.

Crillian froze, then looked over his shoulder and ruefully smiled. "What do you know? You're quick on your feet, too."

"You can turn if you want."

"Even if I tie you, I'm dead."

"There's that," Fargo said.

"Tell you what." Crillian licked his lips. "I'm a practical man. I have to be, the work I do. How about if we strike a deal?"

"You're wasting your breath."

"Hear me out." Crillian's face lit with hope. "I have about four thousand dollars socked away. It's in a bank in Denver. It's all yours, every last cent, if we holster our six-guns and end this here and now."

"We ride to Denver and you go in the bank and withdraw all your money and hand it over to me. Just like that?"

"Easy as pie," Crillian said, nodding. "And no hard feelings, neither. You've licked me and I'm man enough to admit it."

"You want me to forget you tried to kill me, forget all the people you had shot to ribbons, forget there are women and kids in some of these houses lying at death's door because you wouldn't let them have any salt?"

"That last was Jensen, not me. I only did as he hired me to do. What do you say? Forgive and let live?"

"I don't know how."

"Me, either," Melissa said. She had come out the back door and was holding a cocked revolver.

Crillian thrust out a hand. "Hold on, girl. This is between him and me. You don't have a say."

"Like hell I don't," Melissa said, and shot him in the face.

Disbelief etched Ignatius Crillian's features for the few moments it took his life to fade. Then he melted to the earth.

"Well, now." Fargo walked over and nudged the body with a toe. "You saved me the trouble."

"I'll probably have nightmares the rest of my days."

"What about the others?"

"We saw the last two ride to the east. The marshal is watching in case they come back."

"Then there's only one left to do."

"How will you find him?" Melissa asked. "He could be on the way to Canada or Mexico for all we know."

"He doesn't know his cabin was blown up. He'll head back to collect anything worth taking."

"Or maybe make a fight of it."

"I hope he does," Fargo said grimly.

"Do you want the marshal and me to go with you? You saw how crafty he is. And he can be deadly when he has to be."

"He's not the only one," Fargo said.

# 52

Jasper Jensen was throwing a fit. He stalked amid the smoking rubble of his cabin, kicking and shaking his fists and swearing a mean streak. He was so mad, he was blind and deaf to everything. He didn't hear Fargo ride up and dismount, and might have gone on with his tantrum for who knew how long if Fargo hadn't coughed to clear his throat of dust. "Remember me?"

The old man spun. "You!" he screamed, jabbing a finger. "Was it you who did this? Or that damn worthless Crillian?"

"It was you," Fargo said.

Jensen cocked his head. "What the hell are you talkin' about?"

"You dug up the keg of black powder."

"How do you know?" Jensen asked, his fury replaced by a sudden wariness.

"I saw you," Fargo said. "Saw you knife Ramirez."

Jensen gestured at where the keg had been when it exploded. "I came close to blowin' it up but I had a change of heart. Now I come back, and look."

"Time to end this," Fargo said.

"Are you here to kill me? Is that what this is?" Jensen held his arms out from his side. "You can see I'm not heeled. What will you do? Shoot an unarmed man?"

"In your case," Fargo said, "gladly."

"Go ahead, then," Jensen said, and when Fargo didn't draw, he sneered in contempt. "I didn't think you had it in you. We might as well part ways. I'll go mine and you go yours and if I never set eyes on you again, I'll be a happy man."

"I see a rifle in the scabbard on your horse."

"I'm not about to try for it."

"I'll let you reach it," Fargo said. "Let you pull it out."

"Don't your ears work?" Jensen gazed toward the salt lick and the distant hills. "This is a fine how-do-you-do. Now I have nowhere to live."

"You won't need a place."

Jensen chuckled. "You can provoke me until you're blue in the face and I won't lift a finger against you."

"Did I tell you Marshal Bubaker is alive? He'll be coming for you once he's healed enough."

"What are you tryin' to do? Scare me into gettin' myself shot? It won't work. I'm too old to fall for your tricks."

"If it was me, I'd rather be shot than hung."

"You're like a dog with a bone." Jensen casually moved his right hand behind him. "It was a mistake to involve you. Willy and that other one should have let you ride on."

"Willy is dead. They're all dead or gone except you."

"I'll be around a good long while," Jensen said, and swept his hand out. In it was the Colt Dragoon.

Fargo shot him as he thumbed the hammer, shot him as he folded, shot him as he pitched to his knees.

His arms limp, his breathing ragged, Jasper Jensen rasped, "Damn you to hell." Spittle dribbled from his lower lip to his chin. "All I ever wanted was to be left alone."

"You're still holding your smoke wagon," Fargo said. "Give it a try."

Jensen did.

Fargo stroked the trigger a final time. He reloaded, then wearily climbed on the Ovaro. "What do you think, big fella? A night in the stable for you and a night with Melissa for me, and in the morning we'll be on our way. How does that sound?" Fargo smiled. "It sounds damn good to me."

**LOOKING FORWARD!**
**The following is the opening section of the next novel in the exciting Trailsman series from Signet:**

**TRAILSMAN #394**
***BURNING BULLETS***

*1861, the Flathead Lake country—where a tinderbox of hate ignited an inferno of violence.*

The patrol was weeks out of Fort Laramie when they stopped for the night beside a creek that had no name. They'd finished their meal of hard tack and beans and were relaxing after their hard day on the trail. It was then, as they sat talking and joking and some smoked their pipes, that the trouble started.

Skye Fargo saw it coming. A bigger man than most, broad at the shoulders and narrow at the hips, he wore buckskins that had seen a lot of use. So had the Colt on his hip.

Fargo was under orders to guide the patrol to the Flathead Lake country. He'd been there before. Fact was, his wanderlust had taken him most everywhere west of the Mississippi River, which was why he was so widely regarded as one of the best scouts on the frontier.

Private Gunther didn't think so. Gunther was bigger than Fargo, with a square slab of a face and enough muscle for an ox. He was of the opinion that he was the toughest trooper in the U.S. Army and made a point of showing how tough he was by beating any and all comers. The problem was, he didn't wait for them to come to him. He went after them.

Gunther had been needling Fargo whenever and however he could. It started at Fort Laramie when the colonel announced that Captain Benson would be leading a patrol and that Fargo was to be their scout. The men were standing at ease at the time on the parade ground, and Gunther had made bold to loudly remark that he hoped Fargo could find where they were going. No one laughed. Hardly anyone ever laughed at Gunther's jokes. He didn't care. He wasn't trying to be funny. He had issued a challenge.

That became clearer as the days passed. Fargo lost count of the comments Gunther made. They were never outright insults. Gunther was too smart for that.

But they were as close as a man could come to fighting words, such as on their second day out. Fargo had been riding down the line when Gunther loudly declared to the private next to him, "For a scout, he sure does sit a saddle poorly. Look at how he flops around."

Everyone knew Fargo was a superb horseman. It was the troopers, many of whom had seldom sat a saddle, who bounced and flounced and clung to their saddle horn when the going got rough.

Fargo had let the remark pass. He let others pass, too. The one where Gunther said, "I hear tell our scout has lived with redskins. Makes you wonder whose side he's on, doesn't it?" And the one where Gunther remarked, "How come our scout gets to have a shiny new repeater and we have to use single-shot rifles?"

Along about the tenth night, Captain Benson had walked over to where Fargo sat, and squatted. "I'm in a quandary over Private Gunther."

Fargo had tried to recollect if he knew what a "quandary" was.

"I've told him twice now to leave you be but he persists with his foolish antics. I can send him back to the fort but that seems extreme. Especially since I'd have to send a couple of others with him, for protection's sake."

Fargo had grunted.

"So I ask you. What do *you* want me to do?"

"Nothing."

"He'll just keep at you. You heard about the fight he had with Bear River Tom, didn't you?"

Fargo had, indeed. Bear River Tom was another scout and one of his close friends. The fight had taken place in a saloon when Gunther remarked that, given Bear River Tom's well-known fondness for tits, it was a shame Tom hadn't been born female so he could have tits of his own. Tom hadn't thought that was funny, and he'd hit Gunther with a chair. They'd gone at it but a lieutenant had broken up their fight.

"You're not saying much," Captain Benson now said. "But then, you never do."

He glanced over at where his troopers were jawing. "The army has more than its share of troublemakers, I'm sorry to say. Bullies are all too common."

Fargo liked Benson. The captain had enough experience to be competent and was firm but fair with those under him. "Let me handle it. And don't butt in when it comes to blows."

"If I let it go that far, I'll have to put him on report once we get back. It's a matter of maintaining discipline, you understand."

That was where they'd left it. Then, that very evening as they were unsaddling their mounts, Private Gunther had looked over at Fargo stripping the Ovaro, and laughed.

"Will you look at that critter? It's about the most sorry excuse for a horse I ever did see."

Once again, no one laughed.

And this time Fargo refused to let Gunther's remark pass. He bided his time until after their evening meal, when Gunther stretched and yawned and said, "Another day in the saddle tomorrow, boys. I hope our scout's ass can take it. He's moving a bit stiff these days."

Fargo set down his tin cup and stood. Hooking his thumbs in his gun belt, he stepped around the fire and planted himself in front of Gunther. "Speaking of asses, when are you going to get your head out of yours?"

The other troopers froze.

"What was that?" Gunther said.

"You're the biggest ass at the post, so I reckon there's plenty of room for that swelled head, but still . . ."

"You can't talk to me like that."

"As for my horse," Fargo went on, "it can ride rings around any animal in the army any day of the week, not that I'd expect a horse's ass like you to know a good horse from a sorry one. That takes brains. And yours keep leaking out your ears." He paused. "That's what that brown stuff is?"

Gunther colored red from his collar to his hat.

Most of the soldiers looked at Captain Benson, expecting him to do something.

Private Gunther glanced at Benson, too, and seemed puzzled.

"Yes, sir, boys," Fargo said to the rest, "when it comes to asses, Gunther here is the top of the heap."

Pushing to his feet with his cup of coffee in his hand, Gunther glowered. "That's mighty brave talk when you know the captain won't let me take a poke at you."

Fargo glanced at Benson. "Captain?"

"Poke away," Benson said.

Gunther's mouth curled in a smirk. "Well, now, ain't this something? Most officers would be telling me to behave myself."

"You'll behave starting tomorrow," Fargo said.

"Why will that be?"

"Because your jaw will be too swollen for you to talk and the rest of you will hurt like hell."

Gunther laughed. "Listen to you." He balled his left fist and held it up. "I've busted boards with this."

"Boards don't fight back."

Gunther gazed at the other troopers, eating up the attention. Puffing out his chest, he said, "Place your bets, boys. But if you bet on him, you'll lose."

"No betting," Captain Benson said. "No gambling allowed."

"But you'll let me take a swing at him?" Gunther asked uncertainly.

"I'm not *letting* you," Captain Benson said. "I'm just not *stopping* you. There's a difference."

"Damn if I can see what it is," Gunther said, adding sarcastically, "sir."

"Are you done flapping your gums?" Fargo said. "We don't have all night."

Gunther pointed at Fargo's holster. "No using that. I hear you're slick as hell with a six-shooter, and I'm no gun hand."

Fargo pried at his buckle. "What you are," he said, "is all mouth."

Some of the soldiers laughed.

As for Gunther, he watched Fargo set the gun belt to one side and, when Fargo straightened, threw his coffee in Fargo's face.